Smoke
on the ground

Smoke on the ground

BY MIGUEL DELIBES

Translated from the Spanish by Alfred Johnson

1972

DOUBLEDAY & COMPANY, INC., GARDEN CITY, NEW YORK

Smoke on the ground . . . rain all around.
Proverbs of EL CENTENARIO

"If any one would be first, he must be the last of all and servant of all." And he took a child, and put him in the midst of them . . .
Mark IX: 35–36

1

Shortly after dawn, Nini looked out from the mouth of the cave and watched the cloud of crows gathered in council. The three trimmed poplars on the riverbank, covered with big ugly birds, looked like three closed umbrellas with their tips pointing toward the sky. The bottom lands of don Antero, the Rich Man, stretched out black in the distance like charcoal.

The dog entwined herself in the boy's legs and he rubbed his dirty bare foot backward along her spine without looking at her; then he yawned, stretched his arms, and raised his eyes to the distant satiny sky.

"We'll have a frost soon, Fa. Sunday we'll go hunt rats," he said.

The dog excitedly wagged her stub of a tail and looked at the boy with her bright yellowish eyes. Her eyelids were swollen and hairless. Dogs like her rarely reached maturity with good eyes; they usually lost them in the brush along the brook, punctured by the thorns, thistles, and brambles.

The Old Ratter stirred inside, on the straw, and the dog, hearing him, barked twice; then the band of crows rose lazily from the ground with a slow deep beating of wings accompanied by a racket of sinister caws. Just one blackbird stayed there motionless on the dark clods and the boy, spying it, ran toward it, zigzagging through the heavy moist furrows, avoiding the bitch who was barking close beside him. When he raised the spring to free the dead body of the bird, Nini noticed that the oat bait had not been touched and he rubbed it between his small wiry fingers and the grains scattered over the ground.

Raising his voice above the cawing of the crows who were lazily flapping along way up over his head, he said, "He didn't even get to taste it, Fa. He didn't even eat one grain."

The cave, halfway up the hill, flanked by the gullies that the spring runoffs dug out of the hillside, looked like a big mouth yawning. Around the other side of the hill were the ruins of the three caves that Justito, the mayor, had blown up with dynamite two years back. Justo Fadrique, the mayor, aspired to having everyone in the town live in houses like gentlemen. He kept harassing the Old Ratter: "I'll give you a house for a hundred pesetas and you just say no. What more do you want then?"

The Ratter would display his rotten teeth with an ambiguous smile, half stupid, half sly. "Nothing," he would say.

Justito, the mayor, would get irritated and then the mulberry welt on his forehead would visibly contract as though it were alive. "Look, do you refuse to understand what I'm saying? I want to get rid of the caves. That's what I've promised the governor."

The Ratter would shrug his powerful shoulders a couple of times, but then at the tavern Malvino would keep telling him, "You be careful with Justito. That guy's dangerous, you know. Worse than rats."

Then the Ratter, sprawled over the table, implacable, would focus his rough shifty eyes on him. "Rats are good," he would say.

Malvino had been Balbino once, but his neighbors called him Malvino because with two drinks inside him he became impossible. His tavern was narrow and dirty with a cement floor and half a dozen board tables with benches running along the sides. When he came back from the river the Ratter usually went in there and lunched on a couple of fried rats, sprinkled with vinegar, along with two glasses of pink wine and half a loaf of bread. The rest of the bag Malvino

8

kept, at two pesetas a rat. The tavernkeeper usually sat beside him while he ate.

"When men aren't happy with what they have, they stir things up, eh, Ratter?"

"Yeah."

"And if they're happy with what they have there's always some bum that's got to give them more and get them to stir things up. So there's always a show, eh, Ratter?"

"Yeah."

"Look at you. You've got it made in your cave and you don't bother anybody. All right, so Justito thinks he's got to tell you to take that house that anybody would jump at the chance to get."

"Yeah."

Señora Clo, who ran the tobacco store, claimed that Malvino was the Old Ratter's bad angel, but Malvino replied that he was just his conscience.

The Old Ratter, from the mouth of the cave, saw Nini coming up the lower part of the hill with the crow in one hand and the trap in the other. The dog rushed forward when she saw him and jumped all over him trying to lick his rough hand with its fingers all alike as though they had been clipped by a paper cutter. But every time she jumped, the old man squeezed her muzzle absentmindedly and the animal growled angrily but playfully.

Showing him the blackbird, the boy said, "Pruden told me to do it. The crows won't leave his seed alone."

Pruden was always an early riser, and to beat the last week of the rainy season he had planted his seed ahead of time. Pruden had really been baptized as Acislo, but he was called Pruden, or Prudence, because of his good judgment and because he was foresighted. In May he plowed his fallow fields, and so when November came he had already completed the year's cycle. At the end of summer, a little before the leaves turned yellow, he trimmed the branches of the three emaciated poplars on the riverbank and stored the leaves away to feed the goats during the winter. He kept

9

Nini, the little boy, busy with questions: "Nini, boy, is the rain coming or isn't the rain coming?" "Nini, boy, will that thunderstorm bring hail, or won't it bring hail?" "Nini, boy, the night's still and the sky's clear; aren't we likely to get a black frost?" Two afternoons back, Pruden came up to the boy as though by chance: "Nini, sonny," he said to him in a plaintive tone, "the crows won't leave my fields alone; they scratch up the seed and carry it off. What can I do to scare them away?"

Nini remembered Grandpa Román's trick. He used to hang a dead crow upside down. The birds stayed away from the dismal sight, from the motionless melancholy blackness of the earth about to begin to flower.

"Leave it to me," the boy said to him.

Now, as he was eating his sops of bread at the door to the cave, Nini looked at the blackbird with its stiff, steel-blue feathers all ruffled up, lying on a tuft of thyme. The dog, crouching down beside him, was watching him closely, and if the boy didn't notice her, the animal would touch his forearm insistently with her forepaw. Behind the dog, below the hill, you could see the world: a world which Columba, the wife of Justito, thought was unfriendly, perhaps because she didn't know it. A world of brown, symmetrical, gleaming furrows. The autumn furrows, stripped of everything, formed a sea of mud broken only by the bare line of the river, on the other side of which stood the town. The town was also brown, like an excrescence of the earth itself, and if it were not for its patches of light and shadow cast by the rising sun, almost the only ones in the desolate landscape, it would have passed unnoticed.

About a kilometer off, parallel to the stream, you could see the whiteness of the Provincial Highway, used only by horses, by the Fordson tractor of don Antero, the Rich Man, and by the interurban bus that linked the city with the little towns in the valley. A chain of hills as bare as skulls crowned with a half dozen scrawny almond trees closed the horizon on this side. Under the sun, the gypsum crystals on the hillsides flashed brightly here and there with many-colored winks, as though trying to transmit an indecipherable message to those who lived down below.

The advanced fall was strangling all signs of plant life; the meadow and the reeds next to the river were the only trace of green in the expiring panorama. A uniform scale of gentle transitions linked the grays, purples, and ochers. Only above the cave, on the barren plateau, in the oak woods of the common, could birds and animals find a place to hide.

The boy, with the blackbird in his hand, ran down the gully followed by the dog. In the last stretch of the slope, Nini lifted his arms as though he wanted to fly up over the road. The sun was not warming things up yet, and the chimneys were languidly breathing out a whitish smoke. The bitter smell of burning straw spread over the town like a sticky incense. The boy and his dog crossed the little plank bridge and walked onto the Threshing Floor. Next to the straw pile stood the dovecote of Justito. As he went by it the boy clapped his hands hard twice. The flock of doves took off in confusion with a frantic noise of clothes flapping in the wind. Fa barked uselessly, jubilantly, but the sudden appearance of Moro, the dog of Big Wagger, the shepherd, turned her mind to other matters immediately. The flock of doves described a wide semicircle around behind the belltower and returned to the dovecote.

Pruden came out the back buttoning up his pants.

"Here," said Nini, holding out the bird.

Pruden smiled evasively. "So you caught him?" he said.

He took the blackbird by the wingtip, as though suspicious of something, and added, "Well, come in."

There was his rusty plow, his crude cart, and some other equipment leaning against the barnyard wall and over the stable the trap door to the hayloft was open. Pruden went into the stable, and the black horse pawed the ground impatiently. He put the bird down on the ground and while he was cleaning out the mangers he said to Nini without turning around, "What a big beak. That's why those rascals can do more damage than a hailstorm. Damn their mothers."

Once the mangers were clean, he climbed agilely up into the hayloft, took the pitchfork, and threw down a few armfuls of hay. Then he let himself down, took the sieve, and sifted out the dust from the feed by moving it rapidly back and forth. Next he divided the hay between the two mangers and covered it with measures of barley. Attentively the boy watched him work and when Pruden finished he said, "Hang him legs up. If you don't, he won't scare them, he'll just be a decoy."

Pruden dusted one hand against the other and once again picked up the bird by a wingtip and went into the house through the kitchen door. The boy and the dog went in after him. Sabina turned around furiously when she saw the crow.

"Where are you going with that dirty thing?" she said.

Pruden, calm and patient, didn't raise his voice.

"You keep your mouth shut," he said.

And he put the bird down on the table. Then he went over to the hearth and stirred the potato peelings that were cooking over a slow fire. Finally he took them off, sat down with the bucket on the ground between his legs, sprinkled the chaff on top of the peelings, and began to stir it in patiently.

The boy put his hand on the door to leave. Pruden straightened up and said, "Wait."

He followed the boy down the hallway with its red tiles, digging in his pants pockets, and when they got outside he handed him a peseta. Nini stared at him with precocious seriousness. Pruden looked uneasy, raised his eyes to the sky, a whitish sky, timidly blue, and said, "It won't rain any more, will it, son?"

"It's cleared up. We'll have a frost soon," replied the boy.

When he returned to the kitchen, Pruden examined the blackbird with great concentration and then in silence continued stirring the feed for his chickens. After a while he raised his head and said, "I tell you, that Nini knows everything. He's like God."

Sabina didn't answer. In her moments of good humor she usually said that seeing Nini talk with the men in town reminded her of Jesus with the elders, but if she was in a bad humor, then she said nothing, and to say nothing, for her, was a form of accusation.

2

Nini went on down the lonely street walking close to the houses in order to stay out of the mud. He rubbed the coin against the adobe walls, and when he got to the first corner he examined with boyish pleasure the shine he'd raised on its edge. The sloppy puddles were deeper there but the boy crossed over without hesitation, sinking his naked feet in the mire mixed with cow dung and goat turds, in the smelly water standing in the ruts. He crossed town and before he could see the stables of the Rich Man he heard the warm voice of Little Wagger talking with the cows. Little Wagger worked for the Rich Man and people said he could understand animal language.

Big Wagger, the Rich Man's shepherd, and Little Wagger, the Rich Man's cowherd, were the sons of Old Wagger, who, in the words of don Eustasio de la Piedra, the Professor, was living proof that man came from the monkey. In fact, Old Wagger had two extra coccygeal vertebrae like a stub of a tail; his body was covered with thick, black hair, and when he got tired of walking upright he could easily walk around on all fours. Because of all this, don Eustasio de la Piedra invited him around Saint Quinciano's day back in the early thirties to an international congress with the specific purpose of demonstrating to his colleagues that man descended from the monkeys and that it was still possible to find examples of partial evolution. After that, don Eustasio took him to the city every time he had an important visitor and made him undress and walk around on all fours, very slowly, on a tabletop. At first, Old Wagger felt a bit ashamed, but soon he got used to it and even permitted don Eustasio, who was a scholar, to touch his two coccygeal vertebrae without its bothering him. From that time on, whenever a stranger showed interest in his peculiarity, Old Wagger unbuttoned his pants and showed him.

With these social contacts, Old Wagger, in the words of the Eleventh Commandment, lost his way and stopped attending church. Don Zósimo, the Big Priest, who at that time was the village priest, repeatedly said to him, "Wagger, why don't you come to mass?" Old Wagger would look important and reply, "There is no God. My grandfather was a monkey. Don Eustasio says so." And when the war broke out, five young men from Torrecillórigo, led by Baltasar, Quirico's son, appeared at his house with their guns loaded. It was Sunday, and Old Wagger came to the door in his humble holiday suit and his tight shoes and Baltasar, Quirico's son, pushed him with his gun barrel and said, "Now I'm going to show you where goats ought to graze." Old Wagger blinked and just said, "What do you want?" And Baltasar, Quirico's son, said, "We want you to come along." Baltasar was wearing a cross on his chest and Mrs. Wagger looked toward it imploringly and then looked at Old Wagger, who in his turn looked down at his feet and his shoes and said humbly, "Wait a minute." When he came back from the bedroom he was wearing his shepherd's clothes and his rubber-soled alpargatas. "So long," he said to his wife. Then he said to Baltasar, "Whenever you're ready."

On the following day, Antoliano found the corpse at the Bends in the River. When he brought it home, Little Wagger, who was barely a boy, although he did have two extra coccygeal vertebrae, shut his mouth and refused to eat. Don Ursinos, the doctor at Torrecillórigo, said that the trouble was a case of nerves and that he would get over it. And when he did get over it, Little Wagger went up to don

Zósimo, the Big Priest, and said, "Isn't the cross the sign of a Christian, sir?" "That's right," replied the Big Priest. And Little Wagger added, "And didn't Christ say: Love one another?" "That's right," replied the Big Priest. Little Wagger shook his head gently. He said, "Then why did that man with the cross kill my father?" The overflowing humanity of don Zósimo, the Big Priest, seemed to diminish in the face of the problem. Before uttering a word he adjusted his biretta automatically. "Listen," he said finally, "my cousin, Paco Merino, was village priest in Roldana on the other side of the range until day before yesterday. Do you know why he isn't any more?" "No," said Little Wagger. "Well, pay attention," added the Big Priest, "they tied him to a post, cut off *la parte* with a Gillette, and fed it to the cats right in front of him. What do you think of that?" Little Wagger was shaking his head, "But they aren't Christians, sir." Don Zósimo interlaced his fingers and said patiently, "Look, little one, when you blindfold two brothers, whether they're Christian or not, they'll fight worse than two strangers." And Little Wagger just said, "Oh!"

From then on he began to avoid people and to go out on the hills with the cattle until don Antero, the Rich Man, hired him as cowherd. But Wagger liked to chat with the cows and, as people said, he had the gift of interpreting their mooing. Whether it was so or not, he had demonstrated to the most skeptical townspeople that the cow to whom one talks lovingly while she is being milked gave a half a pail more milk than the one milked in silence. On another occasion he discovered that the cow that slept on a pad produced more than if she lay on the bare straw and now he was engaged in painting the walls of the stable green because he thought that in this way he would also increase production.

Nini spied Little Wagger back to and yelled, "Good morning, Little Wagger."

Little Wagger moved heavily like a big, grown man and never looked straight at anyone. Once Nini asked him why he talked with cows and not with people, and Little Wagger answered, "People only tell lies." Now Little Wagger turned to the boy and said, "Nini, is it true that Justito wants to throw you all out of the cave?"

"That's what they say."

"Who says so?"

The boy shrugged his shoulders. He said, "Have you finished painting the stable?"

"Yesterday afternoon."

"Anything happen?"

"Time will tell."

Nini went around the corner of the church. The ruts were deeper there, and the standing water, despite the cold, was giving off a nauseating stink. On señora Clo's garden wall, in front of the church, someone had daubed in tar, "*Viva* the draft of '56." Señora Clo was spiritedly sweeping the two cement steps that led to her stand. Suddenly she raised her head and saw the boy rubbing the coin against the stones of the church.

"Where are you going so early, Nini?"

The boy turned half around and stood with his feet apart looking toward the woman. The muck had left a dirty mark like a black sock on the calf of one leg. Señora Clo leaned on her broom, smiled with all her broad face, and said, "The weather's in for a change, Nini. When do we kill the pig?"

The boy looked at her thoughtfully. He said, "It's early yet."

"But . . . your grandma didn't spend so much time thinking about it."

Nini shook his head decisively:

"No, señora Clo, before San Dámaso's day it won't be good to do it. I'll tell you when."

He continued on his way, and as he saw the dog poking around the house of José Luis, the bailiff, he whistled gently to her. Fa ran up at his signal and fell in docilely behind him, but at the corner she hurled herself upon the flock of sparrows pecking away at the manure. The birds took

17

flight and from the low eaves continued to twitter shrilly. The dog looked up at them, vigorously wagging her clipped tail.

Antoliano's saw could be heard now and Nini looked in the door, open even on the coldest winter days, and from there he saw Antoliano, sideways on his bench, his powerful hand firmly grasping the handle of the saw. The shop was a shack, full of shavings and sawdust, and with a few rough boards standing up in a corner. On the wall next to the window a live decoy partridge kept turning around and around pecking at the bars of its cage. There had been a time when Antoliano earned his living by making two-measure and three-measure containers, but since the Service had started to measure its grain by the kilo, Antoliano had been out of a job, turning his hand to whatever came along. Seen in profile, Antoliano's face exhibited an exuberant irregularity of nose, as if the appendage had tried to form itself of cartilage and then halfway along had given up the idea. In any case, Antoliano's nose looked like a boxer's and because he liked to boast how strong and tough he was, that was humiliating. Frequently, without any one's asking him, he would explain: "Do you know what's to blame for my nose looking like a mashed doughnut? These damned hands." Antoliano's hands, snowy with sawdust, were enormous, like two shovels, and, according to him, as he was walking along one pitch-dark night with his hands in his pockets, he tripped on a stone and landed face first on the rim of Justito's well before he could get his hands out to break his fall.

"Hi," the boy said to him from the doorway.

The dog entered the shack and crouched down in the corner next to the recently planed boards.

"Hey . . . !" said the boy.

Antoliano chuckled without raising his eyes from the board he was sawing.

"Leave her alone," he said. "That won't do any harm."

Nini leaned against the doorframe. A gentle October sun

was now falling upon the street and was reaching halfway up the sawyer's door. The boy said, squinting his eyes lazily at the sun, "What are you making?"

"Have a look. It's a coffin."

Nini turned his face in surprise. "Has somebody died?"

Antoliano nodded his head without stopping his work. "Not from here. From Torrecillórigo. Ildefonso."

"Ildefonso?"

"Well, he was an old man. Fifty-seven."

Antoliano put the saw down on the bench and wiped the sweat off his brow with his forearm. His tousled hair was white with sawdust and all of him gave off a soft comforting aroma of virgin wood. He said, "In the city they keep charging more and more for this. And you can see all it is— just a few boards."

His eyes went dark as he added, "Of course, nobody needs more."

He sat down by the boy on the stone bench next to the door and slowly rolled a cigarette. "Adolfo brought me the seed yesterday. The cellar's ready," he said, carefully running the tip of his tongue down the glued edge of the paper.

"Now you have to make a hotbed," the boy said.

"Hot?"

"First a layer of manure; then another layer of well-sifted soil."

Antoliano lighted the cigarette with a flint lighter and added with half-closed lips, "Cow manure or horse manure?"

"Horse manure if the bed's to be hot. Then you'll have to water it."

"All right."

Antoliano inhaled deeply on the cigarette, thinking hard. He said, expelling the smoke with much enjoyment, "I think that if these mushrooms do well in the cellar, I'll have to put more in the upper caves."

"In my grandparents'?"

19

"And in Mute's and in Gypsy's. In the three of them."

The little boy's look was all disapproval.

"You shouldn't do it," he said. "Those caves will fall in any day now."

Antoliano made a scornful face.

"You've got to take a chance," he said.

The white rooster hopped up unexpectedly onto the wall of the yard next to the sawyer's, fluffed up his feathers in the sun, stretched out his neck, and emitted a hoarse cock-a-doodle-doo. Fa began to jump around in the mud in the street barking furiously and then the rooster bent his head down and began to hiss at her like a gander. Nini said, "That rooster's a fighter. Someday he's going to get you in trouble."

Antoliano straightened up, threw the cigarette butt in the mud, and pressed it in with his foot. He said, "Look, somebody's got to take care of the house."

He was going to go back into the shop when he seemed to remember something and came out again.

"You say the layer of soil on top of the layer of manure?"

"Yes, and well sifted."

Antoliano leaned his head over a bit and before going back into the shop he gave a friendly wave with his gigantic hand. Nini whistled to Fa and then disappeared down the street, toward the river.

3

Señora Clo, who ran the tobacco stand, claimed that Nini's knowledge was inspired, but doña Resu, or, as she was known in town, the Eleventh Commandment, affirmed that what Nini knew could only come from the devil, on the ground that if the child of cousins is simple-minded, there would be more reason for the child of a brother and sister to be so. Señora Clo then argued that the child of cousins is simple or smart, depending, and this Antoliano supported by affirming, "But doña Resu, what is a simpleton but a smart fellow who is too smart?" And doña Resu would be shocked and say, "There you go with your theories." And Antoliano would say, "Did I say it wrong?" And doña Resu would say, "I don't know whether you said it wrong or right, but that's the way you said it."

Well, whatever it was, Nini owed knowing what he knew solely to his observant nature. To take an example close at hand, if the other children gathered around Old Man Rufo, the Centenarian, just for the fun of seeing his hand tremble and then laughing, Nini did so out of curiosity. Old Man Rufo knew a great deal about lots of things. He spoke always in proverbs and he had at his fingertips the saint's name for every day. And if in fact he didn't remember exactly how old he was, he could, on the other hand, speak lucidly about the plague of 1858, of the visit of Her Majesty, Queen Isabel, and even about the art of Cúchares and el Tato, although he had never seen a bullfight.

Nini, sitting beside him on the stone bench at the door,

didn't notice his trembling. Sometimes the old man wouldn't even say yes or no, but he would be stimulated by the boy's expectant eyes, his inquisitive attention, and sometimes by the maturity of Nini's questions and answers.

Generally the old man would start off with the calendar of the saints, the weather, or crops, or the three at once. He would say, "On Saint Andrew's day winter's here to stay," or "On Saint Clement's day indeed it's time to plant the seed," or "If it rains on Saint Bibiana's feast it will rain for forty days and a week at least."

Once the silence was broken, the Centenarian was wound up for a spell. This is how Nini learned to relate the weather to the calendar, the crops with the calendar of the saints, and to predict sunny days, the arrival of the swallows and the late frosts. In this way the boy learned to spy on hedgehogs and lizards, and to distinguish an azure-winged magpie from an indigo bunting, and a stock dove from a wood pigeon.

And the same thing had happened to the boy, long ago, with his grandparents. Unlike what usually happens, Nini had three grandparents: two grandfathers and one grandmother. The three lived together in the next cave and, at times, when he was very little, Nini would inquire of the Old Ratter which of them was the real grandparent. "They all are," Old Ratter would say timidly, smiling his stupid sly smile. Old Ratter rarely said more than a few words at once. And if he did it was with an effort that left him worn out, more than by the physical effort, by the mental concentration it demanded.

Nini would accompany Grandpa Abundio, the pruner, to Torrecillórigo, where don Virgilio, the owner, had fifty hectares of vines and a handsome house with a grape arbor and an uncomfortable barn with a leaky uralite asbestos roof, which was where they spent the night, they, the shepherds' dogs, and the Extremadurans, who at that season were busy reforesting. The first night, Grandpa Abundio wouldn't go to bed; he would spend it repairing the roof with bits of tin and shards to keep out the cold and the damp.

Nini liked Torrecillórigo for the change of atmosphere, although the Extremadurans frightened him with the stories they told around the fire, while they cooked their frugal supper and the sheep dogs snoozed, all curled up, at their feet. They also frightened him mornings with their swearing, when before dawn Grandpa would make the well pump squeal as he splashed water on his hands and face. The Extremadurans threatened to cut Grandpa in two, but when it came to a showdown they never did, perhaps because outside it was too cold.

Once out in the fields, Nini would see the vine shoots standing out black against the turf, and they always made him think of something alive and in pain. Grandpa Abundio, however, cut them without pity and as the useless canes flew over his shoulder he would lecture away.

"Pruning isn't just cutting vine shoots, you hear?"

"Yes, Grandpa."

"Each stalk gets its own pruning, you hear?"

"Yes, Grandpa."

"A green-grape vine, thirty years old, probably has two main shoots, two new ones on those, two or three younger ones on those, and two or three more left on those, you hear?"

"Yes, Grandpa."

"With the sherry or the red you wouldn't do it like that. With the sherry or the red you leave two, and two, and one for the wine, you hear?"

"Yes, Grandpa."

As he finished each stalk, the old man would carefully bury the cut shoots around the bottom of the vine for mulch. The boy took pleasure in his grandfather's work and thought that his obsession with cleanliness came from his profession: from so much pruning the vines of whatever was dirty, useless, and superfluous.

In spite of being brothers, Grandpa Román was the

antithesis of Grandpa Abundio. He never went close to water except in January, and this because, as Old Man Rufo, the Centenarian, said, "In January, you find rabbits near the water." He let his beard grow and every year, around May, he shaved, generally on the twenty-first, the night before Santa Rita. The last time he had shaved, at his brother's urging, was in winter and the man couldn't even bear to talk about it. Grandpa Román would say to Grandpa Abundio every time he found him washing in the bucket, "Get away, Abundio, you smell like a frog." If he was thinking, or acted as though he were thinking, Grandpa Román would stick a finger under his dirty, spotty little beret and would roughly, insistently scratch his head. So, once, when Nini was four years old, Grandpa Román said to him, "Tomorrow you'll go out hunting with me."

And they did, under a quince-colored sun. Once out in the fallow fields, Grandpa Román changed into some kind of a hunting animal. He walked along bent over at a right angle, noisily snuffling the air in through his nostrils, with a club in each hand. Even his beard seemed to be endowed with a tactile sensitivity. From time to time he would stop and furtively look about him, hardly moving his head. His eyes, then, seemed to take on an independent existence. Every now and then he would put his head on one side to listen, or he'd get down on the ground and attentively examine the stones, the clods, and the stalks of the stubble. In one of his inspections he picked up a dark little ball from a flat stone and smiled greedily as though it were a pearl—and the boy was frightened.

"What is it, Grandpa?"

"Can't you see? Roe dung, Nini. She can't be far away. It's still fresh."

"What's roe dung, Grandpa?"

"Hee, hee, hee! Rabbit crap. Didn't you know that?"

Suddenly, Grandpa Román froze motionless, with one finger under his beret, his eyes fixed like two buttons.

"Look, there she is."

24

Slowly he straightened up, stuck one of the clubs in the ground and put his cap on it. Then, as though he didn't care, he moved around in a semicircle while in a soft voice he gave instructions to the boy. "Don't move, son, she'd run away. You see that white rock two yards from the club? See, that's where that foxy hare is hiding. Don't move, you hear? Just look at those saucy eyes. Quiet, son, quiet."

Nini couldn't quite make out the hare, but as his grandfather got closer, raising the other club, he spied her. The yellow eyes of the animal, fixed on the grandfather's beret, gleamed from among the clods. Little by little the boy was able to make out the vague outline of the animal: the nose, the bluish ears flattened along its back, its backside against the insignificant hummock. The hare, like the houses in the town, with amazing protective coloration, was part of the earth.

The grandfather approached her from the side, hardly looking at her, and when he was about three yards away he swiftly hurled the club end over end through the air. The hare caught the blow on her back where she lay, and opened up like a flower. For a few moments she kicked convulsively in the furrow. Grandpa Román jumped on her and grabbed her by the ears. His eyes flashed.

"She's as big as a dog, Nini. How do you like that?"

"Fine," said the boy.

"Pretty neat, right?"

"Yes."

But the boy was not pleased by his grandfather's prowess. On principle he disliked death in all its forms. As time passed he hardly changed his attitude; that is to say, he could conceive as dead only the rats that were his sustenance and crows and magpies because their funereal plumage reminded him of the burial of his grandpa Román and his grandma Iluminada, the two coffins together on Simeona's wagon. For the same reason, the boy hated Matías Celemín, Weasel. The grandfather at least went after the hares barehanded, while Weasel blasted them where they lay, blowing their skulls open with birdshot, without giving them a chance.

Despite all this, Weasel never gave up trying to make friends.

"Nini, you little devil, tell me where the badger is. I'll give you a five-peseta bill if you're right."

Weasel's eyes were gray and aggressive like an eagle's. His skin, burned by the sun and the upland winds, creased in a thousand folds when he laughed, which was every time he talked to the boy, and then you could see his frightening fanglike teeth.

At Grandpa Román's side Nini learned to know hares; he learned that a hare runs when the hunter is far away or crouches down among the clods; that on rainy days it avoids vines and sprouts; that if the wind's from the north it will lie on the south side of the woods or the vineyard and if from the south, then to the north; that on sunny November mornings it seeks out the warm shelter of the slopes. He learned to distinguish the lowland hare—dark as the earth of the valley bottom—from the upland—red as the earth of the upland. He learned that a hare can see as well at night as by day and even when it's asleep; he learned to distinguish the flavor of a hare hunted with a shotgun from one hunted with a stick, and from one hunted by dogs, which has an incisive acid taste because of running. He learned, in short, to discover them where they lay with the same ease as if he were hunting crows, and to discern in the thick silence of the night their rough guttural call.

But also at Grandpa Román's side, the boy learned to sense the life all around him. In the town the people cursed the barren countryside and, faced with hail, drought, or black frost they would curse and say, "It's impossible to live in this God-forsaken place." But Nini knew now that the town was not an empty wilderness and that in every little bit of tilled or untilled ground a hundred living things were stirring. All he had to do was bend down and look to discover them. Some tracks, some cuttings, some excrement, a feather on the ground, suggested to him, without need of more evidence, the presence of little bustards, weasels, a hedgehog, or a stone curlew.

But once, around Santa Escolástica, about two years before, Grandpa Román shaved off his beard and got sick. Grandma Iluminada, who watched over him every night in the cave, was found stiff one morning sitting on her three-legged stool, looking natural and as big as life just as though she were asleep. Grandma Iluminada had annually done the slaughtering for those who had the wherewithal in the neighborhood and she boasted proudly that no hog grunted more than three times after she had stuck him and that never in her long life had she released the excrement when she gutted the animal.

When Simeona's wagon with the coffin got to the cave, Grandpa Román had died too and they had to go back down for another. Simeona's donkey gaily pulled the two biers down the gully, but when they got to the little bridge the left wheel stuck in one of the cracks and the wagon fell into the river. The coffin of Grandma Iluminada opened up and there she was, looking at them calmly, her mouth open, as though surprised, her hands folded in her lap. And down there in her casket, floating on the muddy waters, she looked like something in a can from the market. Señora Clo, who ran the tobacco stand, when she gave her opinion on the serene composure of the corpse, repeatedly said that Iluminada was used to living underground, and so had no fear of death.

When Nini and the Old Ratter returned from the cemetery, Grandpa Abundio had already pulled out, no one knew where, taking along his knives and pruning shears.

4

The Old Ratter leaned down, pressed an ear against the ground, and listened intently to the heartbeat of the earth. Finally he straightened up, pointed with the iron bar to the burrow beside the riverbed, and said, "There's one here."

The bitch wagged her stub of a tail and greedily sniffed at the mouth of the burrow. Finally she lay down flat, her head on one side, motionless, tensely on the watch.

"Watch out, quiet," said the Ratter, and with one thrust he sank the iron bar a yard in from the bank.

The rat rushed rapidly past the dog's muzzle, skittering away with a rustling of leaves, among the dried-out canes on the river's edge.

Nini yelled out, "Get it!"

Fa shot off like a flash after the rat. The man and the boy ran along the riverbank urging the dog on with their shouts. There was a nip-and-tuck chase around through the dead reeds and brambles. The bitch, in her excitement, broke the fragile stalks of the cattails and their spindles fell down on the river, where the current moved them gently back and forth. The bitch suddenly stopped. The Old Ratter and Nini knew exactly where she was from the slender cattails that still stood erect at the end of the trail opened through the vegetation.

"Fetch it, Fa," said Nini.

The cattails moved for a moment. There was the muffled noise of a scuffle and, finally, a short grunt, and the Old Ratter said, "She's got it."

28

The bitch came back beside them, the rat crosswise in her mouth, wagging her clipped tail happily. The Old Ratter took the rat from the bitch's mouth.

"It's a big male," he said.

The teeth of the rat peered out from under its snout in a vain show of aggression.

From San Zacarías' day on, the man and the boy would go down to the riverbed every morning. It had been like this since Nini had been old enough to talk. It was necessary to make the most of the autumn and the winter. At these seasons the stream lost its green covering, and the willow thickets, the cress, the mint, and the brambles formed a dry tangle in which the bitch could hunt. Only the reeds with graceful feathery plumes and the cattails with their black-brown spindles fixed upon the river some sign of permanency and continuity. The thin patches of rushes at the edges were yellowing at the tips, like something dying, approaching death. Nevertheless, year after year, when spring came, the riverbed turned green again, the rushes sprouted up, the reeds put on their lanceolate leaves, and the spindles of the cattails burst, flooding the fields with white fuzz. Then the sticky fragrance of the wild mint, and the buttony flower of the cress stopping up the trails, made it impossible for the bitch to follow anything. The time to stop hunting had arrived and the Old Ratter, respecting the mating season of the rats, withdrew to his cave until the following autumn.

The Old Ratter had no intention of exterminating the rats. On occasions, if the dog took a set on a burrow and he observed at the entrance a few wisps of dry grass, he would call her off, saying, "It's nesting, come on."

The bitch would come away willingly. With her, Nini, and the Old Ratter there was a mutual tacit understanding. The three of them knew that by destroying the nests they would accomplish nothing except to go hungry. The rats reproduced themselves every six weeks and every litter had five or six babies. Definitely, one nest was worth, figuring it low, forty *reales*, which was not to be sneezed at. A similar passive attitude was adopted by Fa if the den entrance was beneath water level since she knew that her participation would be useless. In those cases the Old Ratter had to rely on himself. He would put his right hand in the mud on the bottom, adapting the concavity of his palm to the shape of the hole; then he would drive in the bar with his left and the sudden splashing of the rat as it fled would tell him of its presence. In a second he would feel on his skin a slight viscous tickling and then he would quickly close his powerful hand and triumphantly hoist his prey to the surface, caught by the snout. All that was needed then was a violent tug on its tail to break its back.

On San Sabas' day a rat bit the Old Ratter. It had been almost four weeks since the town had finished its sowing. Señor Rufo, the Centenarian, used to say, "If you sow your wheat after All Saints' day you'll only have thistles to throw away," and the farmers were superstitiously careful not to wait beyond that day. And this year, as if they were obeying a common order, there fluttered in every field, nailed to a stake, head down, the body of a crow. The blackbirds poked about the vicinity for two days in confusion and finally took flight off toward the north. Virgilín Morante, señora Clo's man, laughed in the tavern, "Our friends at Torrecillórigo will thank us for this," he kept saying.

But the crows left and still the rain didn't come. Rosalino, the foreman of don Antero, the Rich Man, kept saying, "If it doesn't rain by Santa Leocadia's day we'll have to sow again."

And Pruden, whose distrust had been sharpened by adversities, answered him that the misfortune was for the poor people, since if you used a machine, as they did at the Rich Man's, it wasn't much trouble to resow. Señor Rosalino, who without stretching could touch his head to the lower branches of the poplars on the riverbank, burst out laughing.

"Only beggars and fools sow by hand now," he said.

That afternoon, Pruden had appeared at the cave very depressed.

"Nini, it won't rain. What the devil could we do to make it rain?"

"Wait," said the boy seriously. And Pruden lowered his eyes because Nini's serene look confused him.

On San Sabas, when the rat bit the Old Ratter's finger, a red sun was floating in the quiet autumn sky, swollen up like a balloon. Toward the town, a warmish haze melted with the trailing smoke of the straw burning on the hearths. A dovehawk hovered over the belltower beating his wings frantically but without moving forward or back.

The boy surveyed the sky along the hills and said, "It just might rain tomorrow."

"It just might," said the Ratter and sat down heavily on the bank.

The Old Ratter opened his pack and took out half a loaf of bread with bacon in it. He divided it and offered half to the boy. Then he cut up the bacon and on the tip of his knife lifted the pieces to his mouth.

"Does that hurt?" said the boy.

The Ratter looked at his calloused finger with the three bloody little perforations. "Not any more," he said.

Behind the sheepfold that provided the manure for Justito the mayor's land, you could hear the tinkling bells of the flock of Big Wagger the shepherd. Moro, the dog, had come on ahead and was watching them eat, wagging his tail resignedly. After a while he came up to the bitch and Fa growled at him, showing her teeth.

Big Wagger was carrying his sheepskin poncho over his shoulder. After looking at the sun he said, "Isn't there a drop of water left in the sky?"

He rolled a cigarette without waiting for a reply, lit it, dragged on it deeply twice, and stood looking at his flint lighter almost resentfully.

"So they think they want to make us pay a tax on this too?"

The Old Ratter didn't even look at him. Big Wagger added, "I'll throw it in the river first, you'll see."

He was smoking standing up, leaning motionless on his crook, his eyes off in the distance, like a statue. The bells of the sheep tinkled all about. The Ratter said suddenly, "Did you see him?"

He pointed with his thumb in the direction of Torrecillórigo.

"He hasn't gone hunting yet this year," said the shepherd without changing his position.

"Malvino saw him," said the Ratter.

"That's not true."

"Malvino saw him," insisted the Ratter.

At the tavern, Malvino had told him the night before, "Watch out for him, Ratter; he'll take your living away. You were doing it before he was born."

Big Wagger the shepherd threw the butt into the river. He said, after much thought, "Get me a couple of rats, you, come on. Seven *reales* apiece, right?"

"Eight," said Nini.

"All right, but give me that male."

The Old Ratter straightened up, stretched laxily, and surveyed the length of the riverbed, putting his hand over his eyes to protect them from the sun.

The shepherd said angrily, "I tell you he hasn't gone hunting, Ratter. Isn't my word good enough?"

"Malvino saw him," insisted Ratter through clenched teeth.

Big Wagger greedily felt the backs of the rats before putting them away. As he went off he said, "Good luck!"

As the sun went down, the man and the boy returned to the town. The haze was thickening over the houses and the sun-baked fields crunched under their feet. The bitch, footsore and tired, followed them. Justito's doves had already gone to nest and there were just a few boys out giving some life to the hardened mud streets of the town with their games.

At the tavern, by contrast, there was real animation. A naked bulb shed its yellowish light over the tables. Frutos, the notary, was playing his endless game of dominoes at the back table with Virgilín Morante, the husband of señora Clo, who was humming mechanically and underlining the ends of the strophes by beating the table with the pieces.

As soon as he saw him, Pruden said, "Malvino, give the Ratter a glass."

It was an unlikely event, because Pruden had a reputation for being stingy. But tonight he seemed all stirred up. He took Nini nervously by the nape of the neck and explained to him something about an irrigation project he'd seen in the newspaper and which would extend to the town. He said impulsively to the boy as he was sitting down on the inside bench, "Think, Nini, it won't make any difference whether it rains or not. Whenever Pruden wants water he only has to raise the water gate and there it is. Can't you just see it? We'll stop living like dogs watching the sky every blessed day."

There was a long pause. One could only hear the noise of the dominoes, and the repetitious tune of Virgilín Morante. Finally, Centenarian with his screechy voice said from the opposite corner, "If projects made the wheat multiply, right now there wouldn't be any room left in our breadboxes."

There was another pause. Pruden was looking fixedly at Nini, but Nini didn't open his mouth. A man at the next table with his shoulders hunched up said slyly, "Give him two glasses. Before the rain comes, we'll have time to finish off the wine."

Outside it was already dark and a greenish, sickly moon came up behind Red Hill and rose languidly up into a high and oddly metallic sky.

5

Around San Dámaso's day, señora Clo, who ran the tobacco
stand, sent word to Nini, and took him to the sty.

"Feel, son; it's already put on enough weight, I think."

The boy examined the hog carefully.

"There's a quarter of loin," he said.

But it was raining, and nothing could be done. By San
Nicasio it cleared, but Nini surveyed the sky and said,
"Don't, señora Clo, it's still too mild. We have to wait until
the sky's all clear."

Since he had learned to talk, Nini had always heard it
said that señora Clo, who ran the tobacco stand, was the
third richest person in town. Ahead of her were don Antero, the Rich Man, and doña Resu, the Eleventh Commandment. Don Antero, the Rich Man, owned three fourths of
the town land; doña Resu and señora Clo, between the two
of them, took care of three fourths of the fourth remaining
part and the last fourth of that was distributed half and
half between Pruden and the thirty townsfolk. This did not
prevent don Antero, the Rich Man, from declaring jokingly
with his city friends that "as far as his town was concerned,
the land was very well distributed." And perhaps because
he believed just that, don Antero, the Rich Man, had no
qualms when it came to defending his property; and the
year before he had hauled Justito the mayor into court for
not boarding up his dovecote during the sowing season.
Come to think of it, a year did not pass but what don
Antero, the Rich Man, raised one or two ruckuses in the

34

town, and not out of meanness, according to what señor Rosalino, the foreman, said, but because the winters in the city were long and boring and the boss had to pass the time doing something. In any case, on Our Lady of the Vines, the town's holiday, don Antero rented a broken-down cow so that the young men might run it and beat it with sticks to their hearts' content, and thus unburden themselves of the hate and resentment stored up in their breasts during the preceding twelve months.

Three years back, because of this event, Nini was on the point of complicating things. And certain sure, something ugly would have happened if it had not been for the intervention of don Antero, the Rich Man, who aspired to make of the child an exemplary farmhand. The fact of the matter is that Nini, moved to compassion by the heartbroken lowing of the cow in the middle of the night, went behind the back of don Antero, the Rich Man, and let her go. Without a doubt his deed did little good, since when the animal came back to the pen, after an eventful capture in the open country, it had a horn shattered, a bloody forehead, and its back literally covered with bruises. But the matter could have gotten even stickier when Matías Celemín, Weasel, pointed his dirty finger: "That brat Nini did it." Luckily don Antero already knew about his abilities and his inborn knowledge and he said to señor Rosalino, the foreman, "Isn't Nini the son of the Ratter, the fellow in the cave, the one who knows about everything and fixes everything?" "That's him, boss," said señor Rosalino. "Well, let him go this time, and the day he's fourteen you get him a job with us."

During the winter, things froze up solid, and don Antero, the Rich Man, appeared seldom in town. Neither did señora Clo nor the Eleventh Commandment appear on their lands in winter or in summer since they had them rented out. But while doña Resu collected her rents punctually in banknotes, rain or shine, freeze or hail, señora Clo, who ran the tobacco stand, took her rent in wheat, oats, or in barley if things were going well, or in promises if things were not going well or were simply not going. And while the Eleventh Commandment never let anyone forget her title of "doña," the tobacconist was just plain señora Clo; and while the Eleventh Commandment was wizened, complaining, and bitter, señora Clo, who ran the tobacco stand, was fat, good-humored and effusive; and while doña Resu, the Eleventh Commandment, avoided popular contacts and her only known activity was the reporting of church events and gossip, señora Clo, who ran the tobacco stand, was a good conversationalist, personally attended to the stand and the shop. Last year she had even gone out of her way to care for a pair of finches, and this year to care for her husband, Virgilio, a blond young man, well-mannered, well-educated, whom she had brought from the city, and of whom Malvino, the tavernkeeper, kept saying that he had found a place to hang his hat.

The boy Nini had had a direct part in the matter of the finches. These birds had been sent, when still fledglings, to señora Clo by her sister-in-law, the wife of Mieres, who was a telegraph employee. She put them in a handsome gilded cage, with blue feeding trays, and fed them on birdseed and millet, and at night slipped into the cage a small warm brick wrapped in cotton so that the little birds would not miss the warmth of their mother. When they were grown, señora Clo stuck between the bars of the cage a lettuce leaf and a piece of tuff or cuttle bone, the first to ease their stomachs, and the latter so they could sharpen their bills. Señora Clo, when she was alone, chatted like a friend with the birds, and if there was any backtalk, she scolded them lovingly. The finches came to consider her their real mother and every time she approached the cage the male would fluff the salmon-colored feathers on his chest as though he were getting ready to embrace her. And she would say mellifluously, "Let's see who is going to be the first to give me a little kiss?" And the birds got all excited, each fighting to be the first to rub his short bill against the fat lips of their mistress. Señora Clo even told them, if they were quarreling with each other, "You be nice to one another now, do you hear? You be nice to one another now."

By San Félix de Cantalicio's day about four years ago Nini had presented to señora Clo an empty redpoll nest, telling her that finches could have young in captivity, and the woman experienced a joy as intense as if she'd been told she was going to be a grandmother. And, in fact, one morning when she woke up, señora Clo noticed in amazement that the female was lying on the nest and when she approached the cage it didn't come to give her the usual kiss.

The bird didn't change its position as long as it was incubating and after a few days there appeared in the nest five pinky fledglings. Señora Clo, aglow with maternal love, rushed into the street and began to proclaim the news to the four winds. But her joy was ephemeral, because a few hours later two of the babies were dying and the other three were beginning to open and close their beaks in great distress as though they had no air to breathe. Señora Clo sent a message to Nini and although the boy in the hours that followed watched attentively over the birds and did his best to make them eat wild silkworms and all kinds of seeds, at dawn the other three little finches died. Señora Clo, inconsolable, went off to the city, to her sister's, to try to forget. Twelve days later she came back and Nini, who was standing beside Sabina, who had stayed behind to tend the shop, noticed that señora Clo's eyes were shining like a schoolgirl's. She couldn't wait to tell Sabina: "The wedding is set for San Amancio, Sabina. His name is Virgilio Morante and he's blond, and his eyes are blue like jewels."

And when Virgilio Morante arrived in the town, young and inexperienced, not much, really, the farmers looked at him scornfully and Malvino began to say at the tavern that the young fellow was a smart one who had found a place to hang his hat. But as soon as Virgilio downed two glasses of wine and burst into song with "The Bellringers," making

Old Man Rufo, the Centenarian, weep for sadness, admiration and respect touched them all. Thereafter as soon as they laid eyes on him they would say, "Come on, Virgilín, tiger, give us a song."

And he gratified their request, or maybe answered back, "Not today, excuse me. I'm not in voice."

And during the slaughtering season, conversations at señora Clo's house stopped having any meaning. People went there only for the pleasure of hearing Virgilín Morante sing. And even Nini, who had been the butcher since the demise of his grandma Iluminada, even he felt a bit overshadowed.

On San Albino the sky was completely clear and Nini went down to the town and walked señora Clo's pig for an hour and prescribed for him a diet of water and bran. Two days later a severe freeze hit the town. By that time the buntings and the starlings had molted, then it was winter and the clods shone bright with frost and turned as hard as granite and the river ran frozen with ice and every morning the town lazily stirred to life under a crystal sky where even the slightest sound cracked out like a whiplash.

As Ratter and Nini, at dawn, arrived at señora Clo's, there was such a racket going on you'd think it was a party. The nieces and nephews had come down from the city and also there were Sabina and Pruden and his boy, Mamertito, señora Librada, and Justito the mayor, and José Luis the bailiff, and Rosalino the foreman, and Malvino, and Mamés the mute, and Antoliano and señor Rufo, Centenarian, with his daughter Simeona. As the Ratter and Nini came in, Virgilio was singing with gusto and they were all listening to him with their mouths open and when he finished they gave him an ovation, and Virgilio, in order to cover his confusion, passed around to the company some bits of toasted bread and glasses of brandy. The fire was crackling at the far end of the room and on the table and the kitchen shelves señora Clo had neatly arranged the onions, breadcrumbs, rice, and sugar for the blood sausages. At the foot of the oven, where the knives were laid out according to size, there were a big dishpan, three pails, and a big shiny copper pot to melt the lard.

In the barnyard the men peeled off their corduroy jackets and rolled up their sleeves despite the frost and the fact that their breath was congealing in the air. Centenarian, in the center of the group, was dragging his feet along heavily and rubbing his hands together as he singsonged, "Tuesday's not the best day of the week to marry a son or slaughter a pig." Señora Clo turned on him in irritation at what she heard: "Stop talking such nonsense. And if you don't like it, go home." Then she went straight over to her husband, who had rolled up his sleeves like everybody else so you could see his little white hairless arms, and said to him, "Not you, Virgilio. You might catch cold."

Antoliano opened the pen and as soon as the hog stuck its head out he grabbed it by an ear with his hand of iron and forced it to fall over on its side, helped by Malvino, Pruden, and José Luis. The little boys, seeing the pig downed—it was squealing fit to be damned, and at each squeal a cloud of vapor formed around its snout—took courage and began to pull its tail and kick it in the belly. Then six men together stretched the animal out on the bench and Nini listened for the heartbeat, drew a cross with a piece of chalk over the heart, and when the Old Ratter drove in the knife with the same force he drove in the iron bar at the riverbed, the boy turned his back and counted the grunts up to three. Pruden yelled, "He's had it!"

Nini then turned around, went up to the pig, and with knowing hands slipped a cabbage leaf into the oozing wound to stop the hemorrhage and, finally, he opened the animal's mouth and put a stone in it.

The men were gathered around him and the women were whispering farther back. Dimly you could hear Sabina's voice, "What an incredible child! Every time I see him, he reminds me of Jesus among the elders."

Nini tried to chase away the memory of Grandma

Iluminada so as not to make a mistake. Skillfully he covered the corpse of the animal with rye straw and set it afire; he took a blazing bunch and meticulously set about burning the hollows under the armpits, the hooves and the ears. An unpleasant odor of singed hair and skin rose up and as he finished, Mamertito, Pruden's boy, and the nephews of señora Clo cut off the creature's feet and ate the knuckles. The moment of truth had arrived, not because gutting the pig was a difficult task, but because at this point the thought of Grandma Iluminada was inevitable. Nini's hand trembled slightly holding the knife when Malvino yelled behind him, "Careful, Nini, your grandma never made a mess."

The boy mentally traced a line equidistant from the nipples and without hesitating took one long bisecting cut from the jowls to the anus. Then as he gently slit the intestinal wall with one single slice he was surrounded by a murmur of admiration. The smell of the intestines was strong and nauseating and he dumped them in individual pails. To finish up he pushed into the body opening two stakes to wedge it. Finally, Antoliano and Malvino helped him hang the hog head down. From the snout a little thin line of blood trickled and started to form a small reddish puddle on the frosted paving stones of the barnyard.

Señora Clo went up to Nini, who was washing his hands in a bucket, and said to him warmly, "You work faster and more elegantly than your grandma, sonny."

Nini dried his hands on his pants. He asked, "Will it be necessary for me to come back down for the butchering, señora Clo?"

She picked up a bucket in each hand.

"Don't bother, I can do that," she said.

She walked toward the house where the men had just gone in and yelled from the door, tilting her head slightly, "Come on in and eat a bite with the men, Nini."

In the kitchen, the guests were talking and laughing about nothing in particular, except for the Old Ratter, who would look at first one, then another, stupidly, without understanding what they were saying. Their noses and ears were bright red, but that didn't prevent the men from passing the wineskin and the tray to one another tirelessly. Suddenly Pruden, for no particular reason, or perhaps because on San Dámaso it had rained and now the sun was out, let out a guffaw and then turned to Nini in a stubborn desire to communicate to him some of his own good spirits.

"Don't you know how to laugh, Nini?" he said.

"Yes, sure."

"So, why don't you laugh? Let's have a good laugh, sonny."

The boy looked at him fixedly, calmly.

"Why, for heaven's sake?" he said.

Pruden laughed again, but this time it was forced. Then he looked at the others one after another, as though expecting some support, but as everybody avoided his glance, he lowered his eyes and added darkly, "How do I know why, for heaven's sake? No one needs a reason to laugh."

6

Nini laughed frequently, though he never was silly or crazy
like the men when they were slaughtering a pig or when
they were getting drunk at Malvino's tavern, or when they
saw the rain falling after waiting anxiously for it for long
whole months. Nor did he laugh like Matías Celemín,
Weasel, every time he spoke to Nini, wrinkling his weather-
beaten elephantlike skin and displaying the threat of his
sharp teeth.

Nini didn't feel the least bit friendly toward Weasel. The
boy abhorred death, in particular violent treacherous death;
and Weasel boasted of being a champion at this. Frankly,
circumstances had made Matías Celemín what he was. And
if he once had bloodthirsty instincts, he had hidden them
carefully until after the war. But the war had cut short
many a calling and had shriveled many a sensitivity and
determined many a destiny, among others that of Matías
Celemín, the Weasel.

Before the war Matías Celemín used to go off to the
auctions in the neighboring towns and quietly bid four or
five thousand *reales* for a stand of pine. The Weasel could
count on not getting his fingers burned in the deal because
he knew how to juggle in his head up to five thousand *reales*
and add and subtract from that the bill for the beaters.
He knew definitely whether or not he would get some profit
from his investment. But the war came and people began
to count in pesetas. At the auctions the figures went up to
twenty and even thirty thousand and these numbers he

couldn't handle, added to the fact that he had to multiply them by four to reduce them to *reales*, which was the unit he could manage. At a sale his head seemed to fill up with smoke, and he didn't dare bid. He began to feel intimidated and to hold back. It did no good for people to tell him, "Matías, things are ten times more expensive than they used to be." Weasel, when he got beyond five thousand *reales*, was helpless, and it was then that he said to himself, "Matías, for a partridge you can get one hundred *reales* without any fuss or feathers, and four hundred for a fox, and who knows what for a badger." And, suddenly, he felt able to think as straight, or as crooked, as foxes and badgers, and even beat them at their own game. And he felt able, likewise, to calculate the price of a cartridge, making the powder at home with chlorate and sugar, and loading it with nail heads. And from that day on his eyes began to sharpen and his skin to weather, and in the town, when someone mentioned his name, they said, "Ugh, *him*." And doña Resu, the Eleventh Commandment, was even more harsh and said he was a bum, and a hoodlum, and a no-good like those who lived in caves, and like the transient workers from Extremadura.

Matías Celemín, Weasel, was in the habit of staying up nights and sleeping by day. Dawn generally found him in the uplands, on the edge of the woods, and by that time he had already set out half a dozen snares for the hares that would be coming back from the fields, a trap for a fox, and a handful of gins and horsehair nooses in the partridge paths. Sometimes he took advantage of Simeona's wagon or the Fordson of the Rich Man to get close to a flock of great bustards, and pick up a couple of prize specimens. The Weasel respected neither laws nor rules and in spring and summer went out hunting with his shotgun over his shoulder as if it were the most natural thing in the world, and if perchance he met up with Frutos the notary, he would say to him, "I'm after varmints, Frutos, you know." And Frutos the notary would just say, "Sure, sure," and give him a wink. For Frutos the notary the outdoors was un-healthy, because the sun fades a man's good health just the way it fades the colors on girls' dresses, and so he spent his free hours at Malvino's playing dominoes.

Frequently the Weasel's cunning did him no good and then he came to Nini.

"Nini, you rascal, tell me where the badger is. I'll give you a five-peseta note if you tell me the truth."

Or,

"Nini, you rascal, I've spent a week running after a fox, and I haven't even laid eyes on him. Have you seen him?"

The child shrugged his shoulders without saying a single word. The Weasel, then, would shake him brutally and tell him, "You damned kid, didn't anybody ever show you how to laugh?"

But Nini did know how to laugh, although he usually laughed when he was alone, softly, and needless to say for some good reason. When the mating season came, the boy would frequently climb up to the woods at night and at dawn when the recently weeded green wheat was combing its hair in the first morning breeze, he would imitate the sharp scream of a hare; and the animals in the fields would come to his call while the Weasel on the other side of the watershed was cursing his useless vigil. Nini laughed slyly and he laughed again inwardly when, on his way back, he would meet up with the Weasel, and Matías would say to him, out of sorts, "What have you been up to, you rascal?"

"Picking mushrooms. You get anything?"

"Not a thing. A damned hare just called from the water-shed, and all the others went over there."

Suddenly the Weasel turned toward him suspiciously, "You wouldn't know how to make the call, would you, Nini?"

"No, why?"

"Oh, nothing."

On other occasions, if the Weasel went out with Mita, his greyhound bitch, Nini would hide along the way to the maze, and when the bitch came panting up after the hare, from his hiding place he would frighten her with a stick and Mita, who was a coward like all greyhounds, would abandon her prey and withdraw. Nini, the little boy, also would laugh then, quietly.

In any case, Nini knew how to laugh at other times, as well as when he was playing tricks on the Weasel. During the spring moons, the boy liked to go out in the countryside, and crouching in the rushes along the bank he would watch the fox come down to the meadow to purge itself, taking advantage of the full moon that flooded the valley with an unreal phosphorescent milky brightness. The fox acted naturally without suspecting his presence. It slowly nibbled at the thin grass on the riverbank and from time to time raised its handsome head and listened attentively for a while. Frequently a moonbeam made its slanted eyes shine with a bright-green gleam, and then the animal looked like a supernatural apparition. Once Nini jumped with a yell out of his hiding place when the fox, squatting on its haunches in the meadow, was confidently scratching itself. The animal, surprised, gave a gigantic leap and fled, sprinkling its stinking urine with its tail. The boy laughed boisterously as he chased it through the reeds and across the sowed fields.

On other nights, hidden in an oak thicket in a clearing in the woods, Nini would watch the rabbits muffled in moonlight, gamboling about in the weeds, jerking their little white tails. Once in a while a ferret or a weasel would appear, and then there would be a frantic scampering for shelter. When they were in heat, the male hares would angrily fight right in front of him, while the female waited for the victor, quietly crouching at one end of the clearing. And once the fight was over, when the victorious male went toward her, Nini would imitate their cry and the animal would turn around, its front paws raised, waiting for a new adversary. There were nights at the beginning of spring when up to a half dozen males gathered in the clearing, and then the fight took on epic qualities. Once the boy saw one male with one ferocious bite tear out the ear of another, and the shrill cry of the hurt animal cast a pathetic note on the silent woods under the silvery light of the moon.

On San Higinio's day, Matías Celemín, the Weasel, caught a handsome fox. About that time the butchering was over, and the holidays past, but the weather continued disagreeable and in the mornings the fields greeted the day as white as after a snowstorm. Besides spreading dung, and clearing the plowed fields, no one had anything to do outside the town except the Weasel. And he, when he came down from the upland that morning, went a little out of his way just for the pleasure of passing by the cave and showing the boy his catch.

"Nini," he yelled, "Nini! Look what I've brought you, you rascal!"

It was a handsome, reddish female fox, with an unusual white spot on its right shoulder. The Weasel pressed one of her teats and a little stream of a thick whitish liquid spurted out. He then held the animal up so the boy could have a good look at it.

"A female and nursing," he said. "She's worth a fortune! If Justito doesn't pay up, I'll take her to the city."

The fleas were leaving the dead body to seek the heat of the Weasel's hand. Nini kept watching the man, saw him cross the plank bridge with the dead fox in his hand and disappear shouting behind the town straw pile.

That night, as soon as he heard the Old Ratter sleeping, he got up and took the path to the woods. Fa bounded along at his side. Under the faint slice of the moon the frost was sparkling on the strips between the fields. The opening to the den was on the north face of the watershed and the boy stationed himself behind an oak, the bitch docilely curled up at his feet. The frost with its tiny teeth bit the tips of his fingers and ears and goatsuckers flittered softly very close overhead.

After a bit he heard some whimpering; it was a sharp

complaint like a rabbit's, but longer and more doleful. Nini put his tongue way back in his mouth and copied the yelping repeatedly with great exactness. They talked back and forth like that at least three times. Finally, in the doubtful light of the moon, there against the mouth of the den you could see the chubby outline of a two-weeks-old cub walking awkwardly, ducklike, as though the airy plume of his tail were getting in his way.

In a few days the little fox got used to living with them. The first nights he cried and Fa growled at him with a mixture of atavistic rivalry and domestic concern, but they ended up by becoming good friends. They slept together in the boy's lap, on the straw, and in the morning they playfully fought with one another on the flat little level area covered with thyme that led to the cave. The news soon spread through the town and people came up to see the little fox, but with strangers the animal reverted to his wild instincts and withdrew to the darkest corner of the cave looking sideways and showing his teeth.

Matías Celemín, the Weasel, kept saying, "I could make money on him, Nini, you rascal! I'll get him away from you."

Two weeks later the little fox was already eating out of the boy's hand, and when he came back from hunting rats the animal greeted him by licking Nini's dirty legs and wagging his tail effusively. At night, while the Old Ratter was cooking a potato with a slab of dried cod, the boy, the dog, and the fox played by the carbide light, wrestling together, and Nini, at those times, laughed freely. Mornings, although the little fox had gotten used to eating everything, Nini brought him a magpie as a present, and seeing him strip the bird with his sharp moist muzzle, the boy smiled with pleasure.

Simeona would say to doña Resu, the Eleventh Commandment, at the door to the church, commenting on what had happened at the cave, "It's the first time I've seen a fox get used to living like a man."

47

But doña Resu would bristle, "You probably mean that it's the first time you've seen a man and a boy get used to living like foxes."

Nini was afraid that, as it grew up, the little fox would hear the call of the woods and abandon him, although for the time being the animal hardly went any distance from the cave. So the boy, every time he went out, would give him a list of instructions and the little fox's slanting eyes would regard him intelligently as though he understood.

One morning the little boy heard a shot while he was hunting in the river bottom. Mad with fear, he started to run toward the cave but before he got there he spied the Weasel coming down the gully with long strides, one hand hidden behind his back, laughing loudly.

"Ha, ha, ha, Nini, you rascal, I'll bet you can't guess what I've brought you today? How about it?"

In fear the boy watched the hand that little by little was moving into his sight, and finally Matías Celemín showed him the corpse of the little fox, still warm. Nini didn't blink an eye, but when the Weasel started to run down the gully, he reached down and began to hurl rocks at him in fury. The Weasel bounded off, zigzagging like a wounded animal, laughing and waving the body of the little fox in the air like a trophy. And when at last he took refuge behind the town straw pile he even showed the corpse to the boy once more, dolefully limp, draped over the barrels of his shotgun.

7

As the winter advanced, the community straw pile got smaller and smaller. Men and women from the town came to it with their donkeys and carted the straw off to their homes. There they mixed it with grain for the cattle, or they made it compost in the stables, or they simply burned it in their Roman-style stoves or kitchens for protection against the bad weather. So, when December was drawing to a close, from the cave Nini could make out, beyond the straw pile, the old frame where the horses were shod back in the distant times when there were some in town.

On San Aberico's day, before the end of January, a sleet storm burst upon the town. Nini saw it coming head on between Flathill and Singmorn Hill, advancing somber and solemn, spitting its frozen droplets over the hillsides. In a few hours the cloud tented the valley and attacked it with its stinging icy arrows. The naked hillocks, silhouetted against the leaden sky, looked like dunes of sugar, dazzling bright. That night the sleet, driven by the wind, beat against the few flickering town lamps and it was difficult to tell whether it sprang from the ground or the sky.

Nini watched the desolate scene in silence. Behind him the Old Ratter poked in the fire. When the Old Ratter was in front of a fire, he relaxed, and as he fed it or spread it, or raked the coals or fanned them, he kept moving his lips and smiling. Sometimes, but not often, he would go out and walk the hillocks beaten by the sleet, and then, as when the goat-killer wind blew, he would fasten his beret with a string, tying the bow under his chin, as in former times Grandpa Román used to do.

In order to be able to light a fire inside the cave, the Old Ratter had drilled through the twelve feet of the earth roof with a rusty old pipe that Rosalino the foreman had given him. Rosalino had warned him then, "Be careful, Ratter, or the cave will be your grave." But he had managed to get his hole through the mass of earth without causing any more damage to the roof than a small crack, which he shored up with a primitive prop. Now the rusty pipe was madly smoking amid the sleet and the Old Ratter, inside the cave, was watching the aggressive and changing tonguelets of flame, lulled by the sputtering of the damp twigs. The bitch, stretched out by the fire, emitted from time to time a muffled snore. When night came the Old Ratter would douse the flame but leave the coals, and in the mild heat from the embers the three of them would sleep on the straw, the boy in the man's lap, the bitch in the boy's lap, and as long as the little fox was one of them, the fox in the bitch's lap. José Luis, the bailiff, prophesied countless calamities: "Ratter," he would say, "any night at all that straw could catch fire and all of you would burn to a crisp inside there like rabbits." The Old Ratter listened with his sly smile, skeptically, because he knew, first, that the fire was his friend and couldn't play that trick on him, and, second, that José Luis the bailiff was nothing more than an emissary of Justito the mayor, and that Justito the mayor had promised the Chief to put an end to the shameful situation the caves represented.

On these occasions, Nini respected the silence of the Ratter. He knew that all attempts to talk with him would be useless, and not because of any natural sullenness, but because the fact of the Ratter's saying more than a few words, or connecting two ideas in a single sentence, tired his brain. To save the Ratter trouble the boy had named the bitch "Fa," although he would have preferred other sonorous names with more of a ring. Only when the Ratter, to loosen his tongue, released an isolated sentence, would the child do likewise.

"This bitch is getting old."

"That's why she's smart."

"She can't smell."

"Maybe, but she can still catch them."

Then silence would return and the quiet patter of the sleet on the hillock and the moaning of the wind would intermingle with the crackling of the fire.

One morning, three days after San Aberico's day, Nini peeped out of the cave and spied a tiny bent-over figure crossing the Threshing Floor on the way to the little bridge.

"Antoliano," he said.

And he waited, watching the carpenter struggle with the wind that was driving tiny slanting droplets against his face and forcing him to bend his head toward the slope. When he entered the cave, the man straightened up, filled his lungs, and brushed off his jacket with his enormous hands. Without moving from beside the fire the Ratter said, "Where you going in this?"

"Coming," said Antoliano, sitting down next to the bitch, who got up and looked for a dark corner where no one would bother her.

"What you want?"

Antoliano held out his hands to the flames.

"Justito," he said. "He's going to throw you out of the cave."

"Again?"

"As soon as it clears, he'll come up, I'm warning you."

The Ratter shrugged his shoulders.

"The cave is mine," he said.

Justito frequently visited Fito Solórzano, the governor, in the city, and called him Chief. And Fito the Chief kept telling him, "Justo, the day you liquidate the business of the caves, let me know. Remember Fito Solóranzo isn't telling you this, nor the provincial chief. It's the civil governor talking."

Fito Solórzano and Justo Fadrique became friends in the trenches during the war and now, every time that Fito Solórzano urged him to resolve the annoying matter of the caves, the welt on his forehead would grow small and turn purple and seem to beat, with tiny little pulsations, like a small heart.

"Leave it to me, Chief."

And back in town again, Justito the mayor would hopefully ask José Luis the bailiff, "What do you think the Chief means when he comes out on this cave business with, 'Remember Fito Solórzano isn't telling me this, nor the provincial chief; it's the civil governor talking'?"

José Luis would invariably reply, "He's going to reward you, obviously."

And at home, Columba, his wife, kept the pressure on him. "Justo," she kept saying, "aren't we ever going to get out of this damned hole?"

The welt on Justito's forehead got big and red like a piece of cinnabar. "And what can I do about it?" he said.

Columba put her hands on her hips and yelled, "Throw that old fool out. You're in charge here."

But Justo Fadrique, by instinct, detested violence. He sensed that sooner or later violence ends up by turning against one.

On San Lesmes' day, nevertheless, José Luis the bailiff offered him a golden opportunity.

"That cave is likely to fall in," he said. "If you throw the Ratter out, you'll be doing him a favor."

To blow up the other three caves had been a simple matter. Iluminada and Román died the same day and Abundio left town without leaving an address. Sagrario the gypsy and Mamés the mute considered themselves fortunate to be able to exchange their cave for one of the little houses on the Old Threshing Floor, with three sunny rooms, which rented for one hundred pesetas a month. But for the Old Ratter four hundred *reales* continued to be a fortune.

On San Severo's day, the sleet went away, and the fog closed in. Mostly it was a stubborn, sticky, motionless fog which filled the valley with strange echoes and which in the deep of night made especially opaque the tortured silence of the barren upland. But, sometimes, you could see it moving among the hillocks like a ghost, lightening and thickening alternately, and at those times the rotation of the earth seemed to become visible. In the fog, the magpies and crows hunched themselves up, became more fluffy and it was possible to get closer to them before they took off grating and croaking, half surprised, half irritated. From the cave the town became a fleeting stage set, ghostlike, that in the half light of dawn or dusk disappeared in the eclipse of the fog.

By San Andrés Corsino's day the weather cleared and the fields suddenly sprouted shoots of the grain; the wheat with a sparse translucent green, while the barley formed a dense carpet of dark green. Under a still pale and wintry sun, the birds stretched in surprise and looked around incredulously before launching themselves into space. And along with them Justito the mayor, José Luis the bailiff, and Frutos the notary, who was acting as town crier, stretched their limbs. When Nini saw them crossing the little plank bridge looking so solemn and stiff in their official garb, he remembered the time when another melancholy group, presided over by a little man in black, crossed the little bridge to carry his mother off to the city insane asylum. The little man in black kept saying with much pomposity Psychiatric Institute instead of insane asylum, but, in one way or another, Marcela, his mother, did not regain her reason, nor did she regain her hillocks, nor did she regain her liberty.

Nini saw them come puffing up the gully, while the big toe of his right foot was mechanically rubbing against the hair of the bitch curled up at his feet. The black visor on

53

Frutos the town crier's cap gleamed as if it were sweating. And as soon as they were all on the little flat area where the thyme grew, Justito and José Luis stationed themselves as though at attention, without taking their eyes from the ground, and Justito said brusquely to Frutos, "Go on, read it."

Frutos unrolled a paper and read haltingly the agreement of the Corporation to dislodge the Old Ratter from the cave for his own protection. When he finished, Frutos looked toward the mayor, and Justito, without losing his composure, said, "Now you heard it, Ratter, it's the law."

The Old Ratter spat and rubbed one hand against the other. He looked at them one by one, amused, as if all this were some kind of a show.

"I won't go," he said suddenly.

"So you won't go?"

"No. The cave is mine."

The welt on the forehead of Justito the mayor lit up suddenly. "I have made the dispossession public," he yelled. "Your cave is likely to fall in and I am the mayor and I have the authority."

"Fall in?" said the Ratter.

Justito pointed to the shoring and the crack.

"It's the chimney," added the Ratter.

"I know it's the chimney. But some fine day a ton of earth comes loose and buries you and the boy, and who knows what else?"

The Old Ratter smiled stupidly.

"We've probably got more," he said.

"More?"

"Earth on top, I mean."

José Luis the bailiff intervened.

"Ratter," he said, "one way or another, you're going to have to get out."

The Old Ratter looked at him scornfully.

"You?" he said. "Not even with five fingers!"

José Luis was missing the index finger on his right hand.

A donkey had nipped it off with one bite, and José Luis, far from being intimidated, returned the bite and ripped off a section of the animal's upper lip. On occasions when there was conversation about it at Malvino's, he would claim that donkey lips, at least raw, tasted like cold mushrooms without salt. In any case, José Luis' donkey spent the rest of his life with his teeth showing as if he were continually smiling.

Justito the mayor was losing his patience. "Look, Ratter," he said. "I'm the mayor and I have the authority. Just in case something wasn't just right, I've made the dispossession public. So now you know, in two weeks I'll blow up your cave, or my name isn't Justo. I'm telling you this in front of two witnesses."

On San Sabino's day, when the committee returned to the cave, a gusty breeze was sweeping the hills, and the wheat and the barley were waving in the furrows like a sea. Frutos the notary was at the head and carried in his hand the dynamite sticks with the fuse wrapped around his waist. As they started up the gully, Nini set the bitch on them and Frutos tangled with the animal and rolled all the way down to the path swearing at the top of his lungs. By then, the Ratter had already talked with Antoliano, and just as soon as Justito threatened him to abandon the cave, he began to repeat like a record with a stuck needle, "In writing. In writing." Justito looked at José Luis, who knew something about law, and José Luis assented, and then they withdrew.

On the following day, Justito handed the Old Ratter a communication granting him another two-week period. By San Sergio's day the time was up and at midmorning the committee again burst onto the cave entrance, but as soon as they yelled at the door, Nini replied from within that it was their house and if they entered by force they would have to take it up with his honor, the judge. Justito looked at José Luis and José Luis shook his head and said in a murmur, "Breaking in; it is in fact a crime."

On the following day, San Valero's, in the presence of Fito Solórzano the Chief, Justito almost cried. The purple spot on his forehead beat like a heart.

"I can't get that man, Chief. As long as he lives, you'll have caves in the province."

Fito Solórzano, with his prematurely pinky bald pate, and his plump hands playing with the desk pen, was trying to remain calm. He thought for a few seconds before speaking, putting two fingers to the corners of his eyes. Finally, he said with ostentatious humility, "If someday soon there'll be anything left of what I've done as head of the province, which is not likely, it will be having solved the cave problem. You blew up three in your jurisdiction, Justo, I know; but that's not the question now. There's one cave left, and as long as I can't say to the Minister: 'Mr. Minister, there's not a single cave left in my province,' it's as though you'd done nothing. You understand me, don't you?"

Justito nodded. He looked like a schoolboy taking a reprimand from his teacher. Fito Solórzano the Chief said suddenly, "A man who lives in a cave and can't put his hands on a hundred pesetas for a house is just a bum, right? Bring him to me and I'll lock him up in the Home for the Indigent without any more fuss."

Justito put his hand timidly forward.

"Just a minute, Chief. That man doesn't beg. He has a profession."

"What does he do?"

"He hunts rats."

"Is that a profession? What does he want rats for?"

"He sells them."

"And who buys rats in your town?"

"People. They eat them."

"You eat rats in your town?"

"They're good, Chief, I swear. Fried with a bit of vinegar, they're better than quail."

Fito Solórzano exploded.

"That I will not tolerate! That is a crime against the Department of Public Health!"

Justito tried to pacify him.

"In the valley, everybody eats them, Chief. And if you just think about it, don't we eat rabbits?" He paused. Then he added, "A rat's the same thing, it's just a matter of habit."

Fito Solórzano pounded the desk with his closed fist and the pieces of the writing set jumped in the air.

"What do I want mayors and local bosses for if instead of solving problems they're all the time creating them for me? Find a way, Justo! Put that man somewhere, do something! But think, man, think; use your poor head, not mine!"

Justito was recoiling toward the door.

"All right, Chief, just leave it to me."

Fito Solórzano suddenly changed tone and added when Justito, back toward him, was already opening the door from the office, "And when you liquidate this business, let me know. Remember, Fito Solórzano isn't telling you this, nor the provincial chief. It's the civil governor talking."

8

On San Baldomero's day, Nini spied above the Nipple of Torrecillórigo the first lines of lapwings winging swiftly southward. For three days and three nights the bands followed one another without interruption, and their flight became more and more agitated. They were flying very high in a great V against the impassive blue sky, calling excitedly with a shivering note of alarm.

In years past the Nipple of Torrecillórigo had been called Moor Hill, but Marcela, Nini's mother, renamed it a few months before she went off to deposit her bones in the insane asylum. Ever since giving birth, Marcela had been ailing, and every time the Ratter surprised her looking with fascination at the hills and said to her, "What are you looking at, Marcela?" she didn't even answer. And only if the Ratter shook her, she would finally stammer out, "The Nipple of Torrecillórigo." And she pointed to the cone of Moor Hill, grim and gloomy as a volcano. "The Nipple?" the Ratter would inquire, and she would add, "There are so many of us pulling on it. It doesn't have enough milk for all of us."

Months afterward, the Old Ratter found his sister sawing a leg of the stool. "What are you doing, Marcela?" he said to her. And she replied, "The stool wobbles." He said, "It wobbles?" And she didn't answer but by nighttime she had sawed off the four legs right up to the seat. The Old Ratter still stood it for a few more years. By that time, Nini had had his sixth birthday and the Weasel would say to him every time he met him, "Tell me, brat, how is it possible for Marcela to be your aunt and your mother at the same time?" And he would laugh noisily, explosively, as though he were full of air and suddenly burst. And the day that the Old Ratter decided to bore a hole through the roof of the cave with the pipe that Rosalino the foreman had given him, and asked Marcela for sand to mix up some mortar, his sister brought him the pitchfork, which she could hardly hold up. "Here," she said. "What?" said the Ratter. "Sand, didn't you ask for sand?" she said. "Sand?" said the Ratter. She added, "Hurry, it's heavy." Nini looked at her in astonishment and finally said, "Mother, how can you get sand with a pitchfork?" A week later, on Santa Oliva's day, about four years back, a little man in black appeared in the town and took her off to the insane asylum in the city, but Moor Hill did not get its name back again and it was from then on and forever the Nipple of Torrecillórigo.

Now the lapwings were flying over the Nipple and Nini went down to the town to tell Centenarian.

"I can't see them, but I hear them cry," said the old man. "That means snow. Before seven days have passed, it'll be here."

Centenarian, with the black cloth covering half his face, was like a dried-out mummy in the sun. Before he put on the cloth, the boy asked him one afternoon what that was.

"Nothing to worry about, just a cancerous pimple," said the old man, smiling.

Any time Nini had any questions about men, or animals, or clouds, or plants, or the weather, he went to Centenarian for help. Old Man Rufo, over and above his experience, or perhaps because of it, had a keen understanding of the shades of meaning in natural phenomena, although the twittering of the sparrows, or the sun on the windows of the church, or the white summer clouds, were not always the same for him. On occasions he would talk about "the wind when I was a youngster" or about "the dust on the threshing floor when I was a lad," or about his "old man's sun." That is to say that in the perceptions of Centenarian age played a role in the impression that had been made on him, at a given age, by clouds, sun, wind or the golden dust of the threshing.

Centenarian knew a great deal about everything, despite the fact that the young men and the boys of the town only came to see him to laugh at his nervous jerking or to lift the black cloth when he was off his guard "to see his skull" and then to make fun of his infirmity.

When that happened Centenarian was in the habit of saying resignedly to Nini, "They're young; that will pass."

Even Simeona, his daughter, had no thought for the old man. From the time that Centenarian began to get old, Simeona took charge of the house and the work. She saw to the cattle, sowed, harrowed, weeded, harvested, threshed, and loaded the straw. And so she became irritable, stingy, and suspicious. The Eleventh Commandment affirmed that everybody gets stingy and suspicious as soon as he finds out how hard it is to earn a peseta. Nevertheless, Simeona was excessively harsh toward her father. On the rare occasions when she visited with her neighbors, she would say, "The older he gets the more he likes his food. I can't do anything with him." Señora Clo looked at her enviously and commented, "How lucky you are, when Virgilín eats so badly for me." For señora Clo, who ran the tobacco stand, now all her worries centered on Virgilín. She cared for him like a child, and if she had had her way, she would have shut him up in a cage and hung it from a beam in the shop, as she had once done with the finches.

Simeona, on the other hand, treated her father without consideration. Her distrust grew with each day and now every time she left the house she drew a line with a pencil on the back of the loaf of bread and put her finger in the cloaca of the hens one by one to make sure that Centenarian wasn't eating a slice of bread or lunching on an egg during her absence. When she came back she would say,

"There have to be three eggs, Father; let's see where you put them."

And if perchance one was missing, her yells and angry words could be heard beyond the houses at the edge of town. And if there was no wind, or as more often happened, if a favorable wind was blowing, the sound of their voices reached as far as the cave and Nini would feel sorry and say to himself, "There's Simeona scolding the old man again."

In any case no one could really criticize Simeona, who, besides supporting her Centenarian father, and running a farm and a house, still had the energy for the pious job of burying the town's dead. For this she used her broken-down little wagon, dragged by the very old little donkey, whom Sime beat without compassion every time she brought a body to the cemetery. To the back of the wagon she would tie Duke, the dog, with a cord so short that it almost choked him. The animal complained, putting his head over on one side to relieve the tension, but if someone said anything about it to Simeona, she would reply, "So much the better. This way even the most unhappy corpse will have at least a dog to weep for it."

Simeona swore and cursed like a man and lately when she referred to the voraciousness of her father she made a joke of the cancer, saying, "The old man has to eat for two now."

Centenarian, managing somehow, still moved about from here to there, but when the sun was high, you could count on finding him sitting on the stone bench behind his house, his eyes rolled up, tirelessly shooing away imaginary chickens. Nini frequently came down to be with him and to talk over his problems or to hear his old stories, into which he inevitably dropped his nostalgic remarks such as "my sun when I was a youngster," "the dust of the threshing floor when I was a lad," or "the winters of Alfonso XII."

Lately Nini had become fascinated by that black cloth which hid part of Old Man Rufo's nose and left cheek, and every time he sat down beside him, he felt an almost irresistible temptation to lift it. His impatience was just like that which impelled the youngsters in the town when, in early fall, the Hungarians appeared with their puppet show in the town square. At the advertised time, the kids yelled out in chorus, "It's four o'clock, raise the curtain!" Nevertheless, Nini mastered the impulse; he worshiped the old man, and in an unaware sort of way, he was grateful to him for his teachings.

Centenarian told him on Santo Angel's day, when the lapwings were flying over the Nipple of Torrecillórigo, that the snow was coming, perhaps in less than a week. And by San Victoriano, that is, five days later, the flakes began to drift down in parsimonious silence. In a few hours the valley was converted into a huge shroud. The whiteness hurt Nini's eyes and the adobe bricks of the town and the thatch that roofed the tops of the barnyard walls stood out against the snow. Life seemed to have fled the earth and an overwhelming silence, like the massive sifted silence of a cemetery, blanketed the valley.

The wild creatures hugged their burrows. The uneasy birds huddled in the snow until the warmth of their bodies melted it and they again came in contact with the comforting earth. There in their holes they lay quietly peeping out with their round wondering eyes, looking about hungrily. Sometimes Nini amused himself poking around the outskirts of the town. The magpies, thrushes, and larks were slow to take flight, but finally at the last possible moment they did, and after a brief vertical flight that seemed more like a bounce, they returned hastily to their beds.

On San Simplicio's day, the boy and the bitch heard the siren call of the snow and they went out hunting. Their footsteps made only a slight crunching sound but in the solemn silence of the valley they seemed to explode with a dull muffled roar. A vast, solitary, and mute world opened up before their eyes and the boy trotted along filled with the excitement of his discovery. Coming around on the other side of Merino Hill, as he started the climb up the slope, Nini spied the trail of a hare. Its light tracks were clearly outlined in the virgin snow and the boy followed them, the bitch at his heels, her muzzle raised, making no attempt to trail it. Suddenly the tracks disappeared and the boy stopped to look around. Spotting a clump of young oak some twelve yards beyond, he smiled slightly. He knew, from his grandpa Román, that in the snow hares don't evaporate or fly away as some superstitious hunters say. Simply to keep their tracks from giving them away, they take a great leap before settling down in their hiding place. So his intuition told him that the hare was there under the kermes oak, and as he went toward it smiling, enjoying the surprise, the hare floundered away and the boy ran after it, floundering too, laughing and falling while the bitch barked at his side. Finally the boy and the dog stopped, while the hare disappeared behind a slight rise, its yellow eyes dilated by panic. Still panting, Nini felt a sudden need and he began to urinate. The dark earth peeped up from a small round circle under the melted snow. A little farther on, he knelt down and in a few minutes had built a snowman, put his scarf around it and tried to get the dog to attack it: "Fa, look! It's Weasel! Go get him!"

But the snowman frightened the bitch, and she recoiled barking, looking at it suspiciously all the while; so the boy made some snowballs and knocked it to pieces. He let out a shrill laugh and the crystal echo over the snow encouraged him to laugh again and then shout again and again louder and louder. It made him feel very good indeed. He climbed the hill shouting all the way, and then he spotted Weasel, the real Weasel, the man of flesh and blood, down below trudging through señora Clo's fallow fields. Nini fell silent and felt a wave of anger flow over his body. The law prohibited hunting on snowy days because the animals that moved about left a trail that was easy to follow and the partridge could only fly short distances. Nevertheless, Weasel was hunting down there and just in case the snow weren't enough of a telltale he was carrying his shotgun low and on the ready for something to jump up. The boy watched him come toward him and tried to get out of his way, but Weasel cut him off. Matías Celemín was experienced at moving about in snow and when you saw him off in the distance moving agilely against the sparkling bright background of the hilltops, he seemed like the only inhabitant of the earth. When he caught up to the boy, Weasel said to him, displaying his terrifying, sharp teeth:

"Were you the one screeching away up there, you rascal?"

"Yes."

"You were having a good laugh, weren't you? You laugh when you're alone, like crazy people."

The boy was trying to walk fast because he didn't like Weasel's company. Weasel's hunting bag bulged as though it had two hares in it. He said to Nini:

"Didn't you see any tracks, kid? Where in the devil do the badgers hide themselves around this town?"

"I don't know."

"'I don't know, I don't know.' I'll just bet you do know."

The boy shrugged his shoulders and Weasel added:

"Justito's throwing you both out of the cave, eh? Where do you think you're going to live, you brat? If you close up a rabbit's hole, he's had it, you know. And that's what'll happen to you for keeping your mouth shut."

Down the hillside came the little tracks of Nini's bare feet next to those of Weasel's enormous hobnailed boots and the light-footed prints of the bitch. The earth, desolate and livid, barely swelling here and there with the round forms of the hillocks, was like a milky surface just about ready to boil.

The Old Ratter sitting on his heels next to the fire looked up as he heard the boy's footsteps: "Did you see him?" he said with repressed eagerness.

"No," said the boy.

"Malvino saw him."

"It's not true," added Nini. "There's not a soul stirring outside the town."

The Ratter's evasive eyes sharpened beneath his eyelids and concentrated on the coals, but he said nothing. The boy also remained silent. For a number of weeks now the Old Ratter hadn't thought about anything but the competition. Nini tried sometimes to get his mind off it, to convince him that the stream belonged to everybody, but the Ratter was blind in his savage stubbornness: "The rats are mine; he's stealing them from me," he kept saying; and breathed heavily from the effort and his exasperation.

On San Melitón's day the sun came out and melted the snow, and as evening fell, there were barely a few thin white patches left on the north slopes of the hillocks. That evening Centenarian finally took to his bed, and when Nini found it out, he went down for a bit to keep him company. An enema bag hung over the rough cot and beside it a dim light and above the dim light a picture of the Virgin. The old man said to him without turning his head, without moving a single face muscle: "This afternoon, before going to bed, I tried to hear the wind blowing on the plumes of the cattails, as when I was a boy. I lay down by the river and waited, but the wind didn't sound the same. Everything goes; nothing ever repeats itself, my son."

The boy began to talk to him about the snow and about Weasel and about the hare bedded down under the oaks, and finally he fell silent, looking at the black cloth that hid half of the old man's face. The latter's breathing was jerky and gaspy and when the boy finished he made no comment. On the following afternoon Nini went back to sit with him, and when it got dark he got up and lit the lamp at the head of the bed. For a week Nini visited the sick man every day. They barely exchanged a few words, but as soon as the day would begin to die out in the window, without any one's asking him to Nini would put on the light. On the seventh night, as soon as the boy turned the lamp on, Cen-

65

tenarian took the black cloth in his trembling hand, lifted it, and said: "Come here."

Nini's heart beat wildly. Under the cloth the old man's face was a bloody mass hollowed out of the flesh and on the upper part of the nose, near his forehead, the yellow bone could be seen. Centenarian laughed sadly and said as he observed the boy's pale face: "You've never seen the skull of a living man . . . ?"

"No," agreed the boy.

Centenarian laughed again quietly and said: "Well, the worms eat us all when we die. But there's no real difference, my son. I'm so old now the worms didn't have the patience to wait."

9

Around San Segundo's day, every year for a number of years the Extremadurans had come to town. They made up a motley group with their string of fancily harnessed donkeys and they arrived singing, as if instead of having just come five hundred kilometers in ten days at full donkey trot on dusty roads, they had just emerged from a warm bath after a refreshing snooze. The troop of Extremadurans lodged in the stables of the Rich Man and they paid him five *reales* a day a head. And as the twelve of them remained in the town almost six months, don Antero pocketed annually about eleven thousand *reales*.

Doña Resu, the Eleventh Commandment, heard them coming and shut her window with a bang: "They're back. God protect us," she said to Vito, the servant girl.

During the first two years Nini went with the Extremadurans to prune the trees on the slopes and to clear out the scrub oak, roots and all. They had done this sort of work in Torrecillórigo, although now they were state employees dedicated to the hard job of reforestation. Reforestation was the obsession of the new men and at the time of the war, barely twenty-four hours after it broke out, brigades of volunteers were organized with the purpose of converting the bare dryness of Castille into a leafy woods. There was no more urgent task and the big shots kept saying: "Trees regulate the climate, attract rain, and form humus, or vegetal earth. We must, then, plant trees. We must make the revolution: improve the countryside!" And with high hopes everybody from all the towns in the valley, their hoes on their shoulders, scattered over the inhospitable hillsides. But the August sun came and burned the tender seedlings and the hills continued to be as bare as skulls.

Guadalupe, the boss of the Extremadurans, who, despite his name, was a tanned, muscular fellow who moved quickly and agilely like a gypsy, said as an opener to the town's young men in Malvino's tavern that they were going to convert Castille into a garden. Pruden had smiled skeptically and Guadalupe said to him, "So you don't believe it?" And Pruden replied sadly, "Only God makes miracles."

The Extremadurans began their work on Donalcio Hill and in a few months they had speckled it with seedlings and made it look like a man's face pitted with smallpox. But as soon as they finished, an implacable sun poured its fire upon the hill and the tiny firs began to wither. In two weeks seventy percent of the little transplants were dried out and crackled underfoot like firewood. The survivors defended themselves for a few more weeks, but in a little while they too burned to death. And the face of Donalcio Hill was again as severe and harsh as before the Extremadurans left their mark there. The crystallized gypsum glittered on the edges of the clay holes and Guadalupe, the boss, when he spied from below the winking eyes of the hill, cursed and said, "That damned hill can't stop laughing at us!"

They talked about the hills resentfully, but despite the sterile result, they did not slacken in their zeal. Sometimes the engineer appeared in town. He was a hearty man although with the paleness with which the pages of books infect those who study a great deal. Whenever he came he met the twelve Extremadurans at Malvino's tavern and harangued them the way a general does his soldiers before a battle.

"Extremadurans," he would say, "keep in mind that four centuries ago a monkey coming into Spain at Gibraltar could reach the Pyrenees without touching the ground by jumping from branch to branch. With your enthusiasm the country will again become an immense forest."

Pruden and Malvino exchanged a knowing glance.

After the engineer's visit—he drank with them as an equal—the Extremadurans increased their efforts, deepened the holes of all the seedlings, so that they would catch the rainwater and protect them from the wind called the "Goat-killer," but the rains didn't come, and when July arrived the seedlings were baking in their holes like chickens in their own juice.

Nini spent a lot of time with the Extremadurans because, aside from their being masters in the art of uprooting an oak or planting a fir with a quick twist of the wrist, they reminded him of the times in Torrecillórigo with Grandpa Abundio, when, at nightfall, in the barn with all its holes, they used to tell gory murder stories. From time to time, someone who knew him appeared in town.

"Nini, kid, what happened to your grandfather?"

"He went away."

"Where?"

"No idea."

"Damned old man! With all his washing he didn't let us sleep a wink all night long—remember?"

But in town they didn't like the Extremadurans because they thought what they were doing was useless; people said they were chasing the sheep off the hills and they were blamed for all kinds of crimes. During their stay the natives enjoyed absolute impunity: whenever anything went wrong people said, "It must have been the Extremadurans."

The Eleventh Commandment went even further. If a twenty-five-peseta bill appeared in the church collection box, or there was an inkling of anything good happening, she said, "It certainly wasn't the Extremadurans."

But Nini knew that the Extremadurans were good people. With their hoes, a slice of bread, and a slice of bacon they did their day's work and asked for no more. Their entire pay went back to Extremadura, where for six long months their wives and their children waited patiently for them. None of this changed the opinion of the Eleventh Commandment, to whom the Extremadurans were under any circumstances undesirable characters. If they were quiet, she thought they were dangerous; and if they sang, then they were bad-mannered. And when she crossed in front of the barn and heard their animated choruses she called Guadalupe aside and said to him: "Guadalupe, the eleventh is: *Thou shalt not disturb the peace.*"

Guadalupe, the boss, stood his ground, "That's fine, that is! And if they don't sing, what are they going to do, lady?"

"Pray."

Guadalupe crossed his tanned arms over his chest and nodded his head up and down, as though he were trying to show that he was keeping quiet so as not to make things worse.

On San Braulio's day, doña Resu met up with the Old Ratter in the square.

"I'm glad to see you, Ratter," she said. "You know the boy's spending all his time with those sinful Extremadurans? Drinking wine and hearing dirty words and obscene stories?"

"Let him be, doña Resu," responded the Ratter with his enigmatic smile.

"That's your answer?"

"That."

"And wouldn't he be better off in school than learning what he shouldn't?"

"He already knows."

"You think he knows?"

"Everybody says so."

"Everybody? And if they don't even know half the mass, how do they know whether any one else knows it?"

The Old Ratter stuck a finger under his beret and scratched the back of his head vigorously. Doña Resu's voice took on, suddenly, a conciliatory tone:

"Listen, Ratter," she added, "Nini has a natural intelligence, indeed he does, but he needs a guide. If Nini wanted to, he could know more than anybody in town."

The Eleventh Commandment consulted her tiny wristwatch and made a gesture of impatience. "I'm in a hurry, Ratter," she finished. "Someday I'm going to have a long talk with you."

The bad opinion that Nini enjoyed with doña Resu was no news, but before the Extremadurans had come this year, the Eleventh Commandment had limited herself to just thinking poorly of him or scolding him mildly. This didn't prevent her from asking him to help her when she needed him, as she had around San Ruperto's and San Juan's days about two years before, with the business of the rabbits.

"Nini," she said then, "don't rabbits have babies every month?"

"That's right, doña Resu."

"Well, what's wrong with this one of mine that's been mated for six months, and nothing's happened?"

Nini didn't answer; he opened the hutch and thoughtfully examined the animals. After a while, he put them back in again and said seriously, "They're both males, doña Resu."

The Eleventh Commandment got quite perturbed and shoved him out of the yard.

Even when don Alcio Gago, her husband, was alive, doña Resu was unbending and domineering. Because of high blood pressure, don Alcio refused to walk a step; but as he was frightened of horses doña Resu had to go to the city to buy those that the funeral parlors were retiring. The nags that pulled the hearses were docile animals, incapable of doing any damage. Despite this, don Alcio kept their gilded harness and the black head plumes, on the chance that if he rode them without these accessories, the horses would notice the difference and run riot. And the farmers, meeting them caparisoned in this manner, crossed themselves because they felt that an animal decked out in such

71

a lugubrious fashion could only bring misfortune. Don Alcio was in the habit of stopping on the top of the hill as the sun set, and there motionless against the light, astride his plumed horse, he looked like some phantom apparition. From then on the hill began to be called Donalcio Hill. But don Alcio, despite his high blood pressure, buried four mounts before he himself died, and when that happened, doña Resu wore deep mourning for him, even refusing to participate in the feast of the first Sunday after Easter. And for two years she attended mass on Sundays from behind the bars of the confessional.

Don Ciro, who was the village priest at Torrecillórigo, and who of necessity said a second mass in the town, was too young and timid to contradict her. "If your conscience feels better, do it," he kept telling her. Don Ciro appeared on Sundays about eleven o'clock, on the Rich Man's tractor, and said a simple mass and tried to explain simply the "Good News." Mamertito, Pruden's son, who acted as altar boy, never played the second bells until he spied from the belfry the cloud of dust raised on the highway by the Rich Man's Fordson.

Mamertito at an early age began to say that before he fell asleep the Angel Gabriel appeared to him. When he was six his face took on a stupid look and Sabina, his mother, said it was because of the apparitions. But two years afterward the boy fell off the threshing sled and expelled from his nose a piñón nut with roots and all, and a lot of blood and pus, and thereafter his face brightened up again and Sabina, disappointed, yelled at him not to mention Saint Gabriel to her again or she'd give him a good slap in the face.

About San Jonas' day, doña Resu sent for Nini. "Come in, little one," she said to him. "Leave the dog outside." The child looked at her calmly and said with dignity, "If she doesn't come in, I don't either, doña Resu, and that's that."

"All right. Then we'll talk in the barnyard."

But they stayed in the entrance hall sitting on an old walnut chest so tall that Nini's feet couldn't reach the floor. The Eleventh Commandment that afternoon spoke unctuously and chose her words carefully.

"Tell me, child, why do you always go around so much by yourself?"

"I don't go around alone, doña Resu."

"With whom, then?"

"With the bitch."

"For goodness' sake! Is an animal somebody?"

Nini looked at her in surprise and said nothing.

Doña Resu continued, "And school? Why don't you go to school, Nini?"

"Why?"

"My, what a question. To learn."

"Do you learn in school?"

"Goodness me! In school youngsters are educated so that when they grow up they can be somebody."

Doña Resu smiled as she noticed the child's mystification and she added, "Listen. The ignoramuses in the town and those no-goods from Extremadura probably tell you that you know a great deal, but don't you pay any attention. If they don't know anything about anything, how can they know whether you know anything?"

They looked at one another in silence and doña Resu, so as not to lose her initial advantage, went on finally, "Do you know, little one, what magnanimity means?"

The boy looked at her perplexed, with the same amazement with which two days before he had looked at Rosalino when the latter asked him from his high seat on the Fordson to give the carburetor a tap because the motor was missing. As Nini showed no sign of doing anything Rosalino had asked him, "Don't you know where the carburetor is?" Finally the boy shrugged his shoulders and said, "I don't know about that, señor Rosalino—that's mechanical."

Doña Resu was looking at him now with a bit of pride

showing, a smile barely sketched on the corners of her mouth.

"Tell me," she insisted, "do you by any chance know what magnanimity is?"

"No," the boy said roughly.

Doña Resu's smile bloomed like a poppy.

"If you went to school," she said, "you'd know things like that, and more, and when you grow up, you'd be somebody."

There was a pause. Doña Resu was preparing a new offensive. The passivity of the boy, the absence of any reaction, was beginning to bother her. She said suddenly, "Do you know the big car that belongs to don Antero?"

"Yes, Big Wagger said it's a stud car."

"Lord, what nonsense. How can an automobile be male or female? Does the shepherd say that?"

"Yes."

"That's another ignoramus. If Big Wagger had gone to school, he wouldn't talk such nonsense." She changed her tone as she continued, "And when you grow up, wouldn't you like to have a car like don Antero's?"

"No," said the boy.

Doña Resu cleared her throat. "All right," she said straightway, "but you would really like to plant pines better than Guadalupe the Extremaduran."

"Yes."

"Or know how many toes the royal eagle has or where the lizard hawk nests, wouldn't you?"

"I already know that, doña Resu."

"All right," said the Eleventh Commandment, somewhat out of temper. "You just want to get my goat—that's what you want, isn't it?"

The boy did not reply. Fa was looking at him patiently from the golden line by the door. Doña Resu straightened up and put her hand on Nini's shoulder.

"Look, Nini," she said maternally, "you have a natural intelligence, but you must develop your brain. If you

74

don't give a little bird food every day, it would die, wouldn't it? Well, it's the same thing . . ."

She cleared her throat stolidly and added, "You know the engineer of the Extremadurans?"

"Don Domingo?"

"Yes, don Domingo."

"Yes."

"Well, you could be like him."

"I don't want to be like don Domingo."

"All right, saying don Domingo is saying any somebody. I mean that you could be a somebody if you just made a little effort."

The little boy raised his head abruptly.

"Who told you that I want to be a somebody, doña Resu?"

The Eleventh Commandment raised her eyes to the ceiling. Repressing her irritation, she said, "It'll be better if I speak to your father again. You're very stubborn, Nini. But keep in mind one thing that doña Resu is telling you: in this world you just can't stand with your hands folded watching the sun rise and set, you understand? The eleventh: *Thou shalt work.*"

10

Big Wagger regularly got up before the peep of dawn and immediately blew his horn from the center of the square. And the townsfolk, upon hearing the signal, pulled sleepily on the cords tied to the latches on the stable doors and the sheep and the goats went all by themselves and gathered around the shepherd, tinkling their bells jubilantly. As for the other, Little Wagger, about that time he was already coming back from the river bottom, where he watered the cattle, and both brothers passed and greeted one another in the square, raising one hand slowly in a friendly greeting, like two people who don't know one another.

"Good morning."

"May God give us a good one."

Then Little Wagger would shut himself up in the stable, clean the mangers, and prepare the evening feed while Big Wagger was climbing with his herd up the hill road, and the first streaks of dawn would usually find him skirting the rise. During autumn and winter, the first people that Big Wagger could make out down below in the valley, among the sullen fields beside the silvery ribbon of the stream, were the Old Ratter and Nini. He could make them out clearly even though they were tiny, and by the way they moved he could tell whether a rat had gotten away or whether they had caught it.

Sitting on a flat stone, halfway up, while he had a bite to

eat, he could follow their movements with a cold and in-different attention.

Below in the valley the Old Ratter stood away from a burrow in a bad humor. "It's not lived in," he said.

The brook, prematurely at summer low, flowed painfully through the reeds and cattails, and on both sides, under a pugnacious sun, the thirsty fallow fields gleamed white, contrasting with the deceptive fullness of the sprouting grain.

The boy urged the bitch on: "Get it, Fa!"

The animal, nose to the ground, was sniffing the paths and trails along the riverbank and as she crossed from one bank to another splashed noisily in the water. Suddenly she stood stock still, her stump tail straight up, her little head cocked, her eyes fixed, her small body tense and motionless.

"Careful, quiet!" said the Ratter, raising his bar.

The bitch took off blindly with a short bark, like a flash, crushing the grass and reeds that stood in her way. For a few moments she ran in a straight line, but suddenly she stopped, retraced her steps, sniffed tenaciously in all di-rections, and, finally, raised her head unhappily, panting and out of breath.

"She's lost it," said Nini.

"She's old now . . . has no nose," said the Ratter.

Nini looked at him doubtfully. After a pause he said, "She's pregnant. That's what happens to her."

The man didn't answer. The bitch jumped up the bank, dropped her hindquarters, and, when she had finished, nervously scratched dirt with her paws until she had cov-ered the small damp spot. Whenever she urinated while out hunting she tried not to leave a trace. At the cave it was enough for the boy to point to the entrance and she would go out and relieve herself. When she was young she did it by raising a leg at corners like a male dog, but after her first litter, the animal settled down and realized she was a female. It was before that that Antoliano had cut

77

off her tail with a single blow of his chisel. But in any case Fa's stub was a happy and expressive stub, like those men on whom misfortunes pile up but who nevertheless keep smiling. Through Fa's stub, Nini knew where there were rats and where there weren't, whether she was happy or sad, where the hoopoe bird and the stone curlew nested, or whether danger threatened.

"Centenarian's dog did it," explained Nini, after a pause, without the man's having asked him.

"Duke?"

"Yes. At night Sime lets him run loose."

The Ratter shook his head in irritation. His hairy chin was stubby and unshaven and he had his beret pulled down to his ears. His eyes grew cloudy as he said, "There aren't any rats any more."

Spring was threatening and the catches were more and more scanty and troublesome. No year had been like this. Usually there were lots of rats in the stream—sometimes up to five or six in a burrow—and rare was the day that the Ratter didn't get a bag of three dozen. Now, with great difficulty, they managed about a third of that. The Ratter said, pressing his toothless gums, "He's stealing them from me." And Malvino at the tavern kept egging him on every night, "The rats are yours, Ratter, get that into your head. Nobody gave that slob any right to meddle in your business."

"That's right," said the Ratter, and the muscles in his neck and arms tensed up almost to the point of jumping out. And Malvino would keep pushing him: "He wants to put you out of business; don't let that bum put a foot on your territory." Then until the following evening the Ratter would spend all his time chewing over what had been said, despite Nini's trying to convince him that rats were like wheat, that some years are better and others worse, and blaming the ferrets and weasels. "They've got to eat something," he kept saying; "there aren't any rabbits." Sometimes the boy thought that the rats might be affected by the rabbit sickness, but much as he searched, he couldn't find a sick rat. Rabbits, on the other hand, were easily found on the uplands, on the paths and trails of the hills, looking as though they had manes, their eyelids swollen, their muzzles bristling with sores. A sick animal was a defenseless creature that had to die of starvation: blind and with no sense of smell, it was incapable of finding food.

Nini dug out a cave with a nest and called the Ratter over. "Look," he said.

In the straw two tiny pink bodies were wriggling. Their eyes were still closed, but, by contrast, their mouths were exceptionally large and open.

"There, see, two babies," added the boy. "Nobody's to blame."

Ordinarily, the rat litters were five to eight. The Ratter said, after looking at them closely, "They were born tonight."

The boy covered the nest, taking care not to hurt them. He insisted, "It's leap year. Nobody's to blame."

On the following morning, when they were lying in wait for the otter in the river bottom, Nini stumbled on the ratter from Torrecillórigo. He was a well-built young man, with lively eyes, a determined look, and was wearing a brown corduroy jacket and hobnailed boots like Weasel's. His dog was sniffing in the grass half-heartedly. The man smiled at the boy and said as he squatted down, sticking his bar into the ground, "What's going on that there aren't any rats this year?"

"How do I know?" said the boy.

"Last year there were loads of them."

"Not this year. The weasels are hunting them, and the ferrets."

"Ferrets too?"

"Just look. There aren't any rabbits up there. The sickness has cleaned them out. They've got to eat something."

Then he didn't say a word for a bit, as he sat next to the river observing the man. Fa also watched what he was doing, and from time to time, growled with unconcealed ill will. Nini saw the flabby bag on the man's belt.

"You didn't catch anything?"

The other smiled; his smile was very white in contrast with his tanned face: "I didn't see any either."

The boy put his elbows on his knees, his head in his hands. "Why do you do it?" he asked at last.

"Why do I do what?"

"Hunt rats."

"To pass the time. Look, I like rats."

"Do you sell them?"

The other burst out laughing heartily.

"That's a good one. If I get enough for a meal, I'm satisfied," he said.

Then the boy suggested he hunt inside the limits of Torrecillórigo. The young man seemed very amused: "Is this posted?"

The boy said nothing. The man sat down on the riverbank, rolled a cigarette, lit it, and stretched out in the sun. He was squinting his eyes, either from the cigarette smoke or from the force of the sun, and suddenly he sat up and said, "Seems it doesn't want to rain."

Pruden, since San Juan Clímaco's day, had kept saying every evening at Malvino's tavern, "If it doesn't rain by San Quinciano, it'll be bad, by God." Rosalino and Virgilio and José Luis and Justito and Guadalupe and all the men in the town didn't say anything, but every morning they looked up and when all they saw was blue sky they muttered curses and swore under their breath. Nevertheless, they got their tools and they went out to cultivate the seeded fields as the sun rose or to give a second plowing to the fallow fields, and when they finished they sat down in silence in the tavern to wait for rain, and, if they could, tried to forget the danger and said, "Come on, Virgilio, give it a go. At least we can have some music."

The same sort of thing happened in September when they were patiently waiting for it to rain so they could get the harvest in. The men in the town tried to protect themselves against adversity and they marked out the course of the year with feast days and pilgrimages. But rain or hail or plant lice or a black frost always came and upset everything. Around March Sunday, which this year fell on San Porfirio's day, the town looked like a funeral. Nevertheless, the young men divided themselves up as usual into two choruses and both fought to get Virgilio Morante on their side. But shortly after they lit the bonfires señora Clo appeared and said there was a slight drizzle and that Virgilio had a cold and should stay at home. The choruses, without Virgilio, could hardly find the right notes and the girls laughed from the windows at their dissonant efforts. Then in the pantries there weren't enough rats for everybody and once more there was fulfillment of Centenarian's prophecy: "Wine in plenty, meat for just twenty." And José Luis said brutally to the Old Ratter, "You're through; you'll have to apply to the rest home." And the Ratter said, "There aren't any more rats; he's stealing them on me."

Hardly had Nini gotten back from his spying on the otter when the Ratter said to him mechanically, "Did you see him?"

The boy didn't answer. The Old Ratter raised his eyes from his soup plate. "Did you see him?" he insisted.

The boy still didn't answer right away. "He doesn't know," he said finally. "And his dog doesn't either."

The Ratter grabbed him by the hair and forced him to raise his head. "Where was he, tell me."

The boy's mouth twisted in an expression of pain. "Down at the Bends," he said. "But he doesn't know. All afternoon he just caught one rat, see."

The Old Ratter let him go, but his fingers were still clutched, and finally he joined them with those of the other hand as though he were squeezing someone's throat and he said, "If I catch him, I'll kill him."

Then he stood there breathing heavily from the effort.

On San Andrés Hivernón's day, the bitch lost an eye. It

happened the same day that Big Wagger the shepherd used his stick to kill a five-foot snake that was milking Pruden's she-goat after hypnotizing it. Fa had her accident because the Old Ratter was anxious; he was too eager to have her hunt through the reeds and brush and brambles. The Old Ratter was tireless: "Go get him, sic him!" he kept saying. And the animal obediently followed the trails through the tangle of weeds and nettles.

When she came out of the brush with her damaged eye she was whimpering slightly. The Old Ratter said, "She's through; she's old." And the boy took her in his arms and spent the whole night applying compresses of aloe and pepper. On the following morning he bathed her eye with plum juice, but nothing helped; the bitch was now blind in one eye and had a funny expression on her face, half roguish, half taciturn.

On San Juan de Ante Portam Latinam's day the bitch had her pups; there were six speckled ones and one cinnamon-colored. Nini went down to see Centenarian and give him the good news.

"Now we're related, right?" the old man said to him.

"Related, señor Rufo?"

"Let's see . . . don't the pups belong to Duke and your bitch?"

"Yes."

"Well, then."

The boy couldn't get used to being alone now. He missed the bitch beside him. Every time he left the cave, the little dog watched him with her one eye, hesitating between leaving him and leaving her babies. One afternoon when he came back from his forays, he found her howling sorrowfully. Under her, hidden in her teats, the cinnamon pup was playing all alone. The Ratter said with a crafty smile, "He can see all right."

Nini looked at him without answering. The Old Ratter added, "He's got good sharp eyes."

The boy hesitated. "And the others?" he finally said.

"The others?"

"Where did you put them?"

The Old Ratter's face twisted in a stupid, sly grin: "Where? Over there."

The bitch was whimpering at his side and Nini took the pup in his arms and went out of the cave. Fa went on ahead following the track down the gully, crossed the road, and along the edge of the wheatfield, reached the meadow, raised her muzzle to the wind and finally, without hesitating, went straight to the river. Once there she lay down, hanging her head, as though overcome. Then Nini glimpsed among the cattails the first pup. One by one he picked up the six corpses and right there in the meadow he dug a deep hole and buried them. When he finished he put a cross of sticks over the mound and Fa hunched up beside it looking at him dimly with her one grateful eye.

11

The storks almost never migrated back on the same day of the month. But this did not prevent Nini from announcing their arrival a few days ahead. In the valley there had existed for years the belief that the stork was a herald of spring, although in reality, at San Blas' day, the date they ordinarily appeared, the hard winter on the meseta was barely half over. Centenarian was in the habit of saying, "In Castille, you know, nine months of ice and snow, and three of hell's inferno." And rare was the year that he was wrong.

Nini knew that the storks that nested in the tower were always the same ones and not their offspring, because one year he banded them and the following year they came back with their usual punctuality and the rings shone brightly in the sun like gold on the tip top of the belltower. Some time back Nini had made a habit of climbing up the belltower each spring, on the Sunday after Easter; and from the top of the tower under the twigs of the nest he would watch in fascination the transformation of the earth. At that time of year, the town was stirring out of its winter limbo, and as its drooping vitality gathered strength it took on a false appearance of fertility. The wheat made a green carpet which gradually lost color off in the distance bounded by the chain of hills, whose arid crests were softened by the dull green of thyme and furze, the watery blue of lavender, and the deep purple of sage. Nevertheless the hilltops continued to display their grim faces, which stood out against the changing iridescence of the crystallized gypsum and the resigned look of the flock of Big Wagger the shepherd, as it obstinately browsed among the cracks and stones on the scraggly upland plants.

Beneath the belfry the town spread out, bounded by the stream, the provincial highway, the straw pile, and the stables of don Antero the Rich Man. The creek reflected and reverberated the trembling rigidity of the three poplars on the riverbank whose mutilated branches were starting to show green again. On the other side of the river the boy could make out his cave, tiny in the distance, like a cricket's burrow, and on the turn of the hill, the tumbled-in caves of his grandparents, of Sagrario the gypsy, and Mamés the mute. Farther back there rose the community oak grove, and the eagles and mousehunters flew above it constantly spying for their food. It was, all of it, like a portentous resurrection, and when the day of Saint Augustine's conversion arrived, the growth along the stream was shooting up again matted and rough; the strips between the fields were crowding with poppies and daisies; violets and bunches of wild yellow flowers were swelling the damp gullies; and the crickets were knifing the silence of the valley with irritating persistence.

Nevertheless, this year, the weather continued harsh on Santa María Cleofé's day, despite the calendar's official announcement of springtime two weeks before. Some high clouds, barely tinged with sooty black, furrowed the sky swiftly, but the north wind did not weaken and hopes of rain were vanishing. Next to the stream, on the tiny bits of land the water could reach, the men sowed escarole, Swiss chard, artichokes, and dwarf peas. Others cut down the grain on the highland for green fodder and prepared the sowing of short-cycle wheat. The mares were bred, and with the milk from the she-goats and the sheep they made cheeses for the market at Torrecillórigo. In the hives that had been recently set up, they let in ventilation to prevent premature swarming, and Nini was kept so busy that he simply couldn't attend to all the requests of his fellow townsfolk.

"Nini, look, I want to get some new bee colonies. If I don't get wheat, at least I may get some honey."

"Nini, is it true that if I don't destroy the queen cells the swarm will get away from me? And how in the devil am I going to know which are the queen cells?"

And Nini attended to all of them with his usual solicitude.

On San Lamberto's day, the clouds scattered and the ceiling lifted, and over the grain fields there began to form whitish rings. Pruden gave the alarm one night at the tavern.

"Now the bugs are here!" he said. "The copper sulphate can't control them."

Silence answered him. For about two weeks there hadn't been a sound in the town except for the sinister rattling of the storks on the top of the tower, and the mournful bleating of the new lambs behind the barnyard walls. Men and women walked along the dirty streets dragging their feet in the dust, their faces somber, as though expecting a disaster. They knew the bugs too well to be optimistic. The year of the famine, the "rooster's eye" leveled the fields, and two years later the "cyclonium" didn't respect one single stalk. The men in the town said "cyclonium," mechanically making a cross with their fingers, just as they saw don Ciro do every time he tossed a few Latin words from the church pulpit. To the more religious townsfolk it seemed blasphemous that such a cruel and destructive parasite should be called "cyclonium." Nevertheless, whether the name was right or not, the "cyclonium" took it out on them, or at least threatened to, every year in the month of April. Old Man Rufo repeatedly said, "April is a time to fear, the loss of the whole year." And in the depths of their hearts the men of the town harbored a concentrated hate for this versatile and capricious month.

On San Fidel de Sigmaringa's day, seeing that the drought was continuing, doña Resu proposed they take out the saint to beg rain from On High, although don Ciro, the parish priest of Torrecillórigo, with his excessive youth and humility and his indecisive timidity, didn't seem to the men of the town effective enough for such a transcendental need. About don Ciro it was said that the day Yayo the blacksmith of Torrecillórigo beat his mother to death, buried her under a pile of manure, and came to him to unload his sins, don Ciro absolved him and said to him gently, "Pray three Hail Marys, my son, with great feeling, and don't do it again."

With all this, more and more everyone missed don Zósimo the Big Priest. Don Zósimo the Big Priest stood seven and one half feet tall and weighed 275 pounds. He was a jovial man who never stopped growing. Nini's mother, la Marcela, used his name to frighten the boy: "If you're not quiet," she would say to him, "I'll take you to the Big Priest's to see him snore." And Nini was quiet, because that gigantic man, wrapped in black, with that big thundering voice, scared him to death. And when they had a procession to ask God to rain, the Big Priest didn't seem to pray but rather to demand. He would say, "Lord, grant us a helpful rain and make the celestial waters flow over the thirsty face of the earth," as though he were talking to an equal in a confidential conversation. And with that thundering voice even the hills seemed to tremble and be moved.

By contrast, don Ciro got down on his knees in the dust at the Stone Cross, and said, bowing his head and opening his weak arms, "Appease, O Lord, your anger with the gifts we offer you and send us the help we need of an abundant rain." And his voice was as weak as his arms, and the townsfolk had no faith that such a slender prayer would find any answer On High. And it was the same sort of thing with the mission sermons. Every time don Zósimo the Big Priest mounted the pulpit, he talked to them about fornication, and hellfire. And he orated with a voice that seemed to come from beyond the grave, and when he finished his last sermon, the men and women left the church soaked in sweat, just as if for a few days they had shared with the reprobates the fiery pains of hell. By contrast, don Ciro spoke softly, with a reflective warm tenderness, of a God near and compassionate, and of social justice and distributive justice and commutative justice, but they hardly understood any of this and if they took those talks, it was just because when they left church, during the summer, don Antero the Rich Man and Mamel, the elder son of don Antero, went into a towering rage against priests who played politics and stuck their noses in where they didn't belong.

Nevertheless the town went in a body to form the procession. Before the break of dawn, just as soon as Antoliano's white rooster crowed his hoarse cock-a-doodle-doo from the barnyard fence, two dark lines clumsily took form and moved off, oh so slowly, following the uncertain lines of the ruts. Step by step men and women walked along praying the dawn rosary and at each Station of the Cross they made a halt; and then they could hear the sweet tinkling of Big Wagger's sheep from the slopes above. And as if this were the signal, the town then intoned out of tune, sorrowfully, the "Forgive us, O Lord." That's how it went until they reached the Stone Cross on the hill, before which don Ciro humbly prostrated himself and said, "Appease, O Lord, your anger with the gifts we offer you and send us the help we need of an abundant rain." And so it was day after day.

On San Celestino and San Anastasio's day the processions ended. The sky continued clear, each day a little more intensely blue than the day before. Nevertheless, when the sun went down, Nini observed that as the smoke from the cave left the pipe it blew down the ravine and wound along the slope of their hill like a snake. Without giving it a moment's more thought, he turned around and rushed headlong down the gully, his arms outstretched as though he were flying. On the little bridge next to the stream he could see Pruden bending down over his field.

"Pruden!" he shouted excitedly, and pointed a finger at

the chimney halfway up the rise. "Smoke on the ground, rain all around. It'll rain tomorrow."

And Pruden raised his sweaty face and, startled, looked at him as though he were a ghost, then he immediately stuck his hoe in the earth and without answering a word rushed off like a madman through the town streets, waving his arms on high and yelling like a man possessed, "It's going to rain! Nini said so! It's going to rain!"

And the men interrupted their chores and smiled to themselves and the women appeared at the openings in the walls of the houses murmuring, "May his mouth be an angel," and the children and the dogs, caught up in the excitement, ran excitedly after Pruden and they all shouted as loud as they could, "It's going to rain! Tomorrow it will rain! Nini said so!"

At the tavern the wine flowed that night. The menfolk were exultant and even Mamés the mute was determined to communicate his good spirits by constantly brushing his fingers over his mouth in a sign of glee. But impatience prevented the men of the town from translating his language and Mamés made livelier and livelier motions until Antoliano told him, "Mute, don't yell like that! I'm not deaf." And everyone, even Mamés, burst out laughing and, after a bit, Virgilín began to sing "The Daughter of Juan Simón" and everybody was quiet because Virgilín put his heart into it, and only Pruden nudged José Luis with his elbow and mused, "Hey, you, today he's singing like an angel."

On the following day, the Resurrection of the Holy Cross, a dark gray cloud settled down over Donalcio Hill, moving very slowly toward the southeast.

And Nini, right after getting up, scrutinized it attentively. Finally he turned to the Ratter and said, "The rain's here."

And with the rain the wind burst upon them and during the night it howled lugubriously as it lashed the hilltops. The roar of the hurricane unsettled the boy. It seemed to him that the dead from the little cemetery, led by Grandma

Iluminada and Grandpa Román, and the hares and the foxes and the badgers and the birds killed by Matías Celemín the Weasel were swarming together over the town to settle accounts. But this time the wind limited itself to scattering the big cloud over the valley and then calmed down. It was a dense leaden cloud that looked like a mole's belly and for three days and three nights it poured rain on the region. And the men, sitting in the doorways of their houses, let the rain wet them while they jubilantly rubbed their calloused hands and said, squinting sharply at the sky, "That's the water we needed. This year it came on time."

On the morning of the fourth day, silence wakened Nini. The boy looked out the mouth of the cave and saw that the cloud had passed and a timid ray of sunlight was pushing through its last straggling white locks, projecting a luminous rainbow from Donalcio Hill to Red Mountain. The soft smell of the intoxicated earth reached the boy and as soon as he heard the nightingale sing down below among the willows he knew that spring had come.

12

From San Gregorio Nacianceno's day on, the song of the crickets in the valley became a veritable racket. It was like a multiple obstinate screeching that impressed on the fields, on the slow-moving river, on the wretched mud and straw huts, and on the sullen hilltops that festooned the horizon a kind of nervous vibration that spread out in growing waves, like a tide, at dusk and at dawn, only to calm down toward the middle of the day or the middle of the night. In any case the song of the crickets had a volume and a density, it filtered through every crack and set up a strident background for every chore, but the men and women of the town paid no attention to it; it was a something, like air or bread, that had its own vital rhythm without their being aware of it. Only Columba, Justito's wife, would sometimes go up to her husband with her open hands nervously clutched over her breast, and sob, "Those crickets, Justo. Those crickets make it impossible to breathe."

Beyond that, the appearance of the crickets signified for the town the beginning of a long wait. The crop fields, harrowed and weeded, waved green in the distance like a firm promise, and the men looked at the sky insistently, since the sky was the source of water and thirst, of freezes and bugs; and definitely, at this point, only from On High could they hope for the grain to form on the stalks and for the success of the harvest.

With the appearance of the crickets, Columba, Justito's wife, was in the habit of calling on Nini to take the chicks from the hen and put them with the capon. Ordinarily she didn't pay him for this job, because, according to Columba, money in boys' pockets only served to lead them astray; she limited herself to giving him a chocolate candy and a piece of bread for lunch, and then she talked with him from a distance, next to the well, and as soon as Nini went away a feeling of discomfort came over her, like an insubstantial prickling that spread over her whole body. The fact of the matter was that this happened to her every time she got close to any of her fellow townsfolk, and because of it Columba ended up by avoiding everybody. In truth, Columba longed for her childhood in a suburb of the city and she couldn't come to terms with the silence of the town, nor with the dust of the town, nor with the dirtiness of the town, nor with the primitivism of the town. Columba demanded, at least, running water, paved streets and a movie theater and any kind of a place to dance and kill time. She kept Justito, her husband, busy.

"Justo," she would say to him, "as soon as I get out of bed, just seeing nothing around makes me want to throw up."

Justito got upset: "And where better can we go?"

Columba's eyes would turn very white. "To hell! Anywhere! Didn't Quinciano leave?"

"He's a fine example, Quinciano is. Day laborer in Bilbao and dying of starvation."

"Better dead of starvation in Bilbao than dead of too much to eat here in this god-forsaken place."

For Columba, the town was a barren waste and the arrival of the hoopoes, the swallows, and the swifts didn't change in the least little bit her point of view. Nor was it changed by the coming of the quail, the azure-winged magpies, the bee-eaters, or the doves flying in thick flocks at an altitude of six thousand feet. Nor was it changed by the frantic clacking of the goatsuckers, the monotonous and penetrating concert of the crickets in the crop fields, nor the dry barking of the snowy owl.

With Nini, Columba simply had nothing in common. He

struck her as just one more product of that wretched earth, and every time she met him she would look at him with scorn and suspicion. Which is why Columba went to Nini for help only when there was no other way—as when she had to take the combs from the hive, or castrate the boar or take the chicks from the hen and put them with the capon. But ordinarily she put on Justito the burden of her loneliness and defenselessness.

"All right, what about Longinos? Didn't Longinos leave? And who was worse off than he was around here?"

"That's something else again. Longinos went off to León to his sister's. He had a table all set and waiting for him."

"That's right, sure. Everybody has his reasons except us."

Nevertheless, every time Fito Solórzano the Chief spoke to him about the caves, Justito the mayor could see a speck of light rise on the horizon.

"If the Chief would help me . . . ," he would say. "But first I have to put an end to the caves."

Columba would get all excited: "If it were up to me I wouldn't just go around thinking about it."

"You . . . you . . . you think you can fix everything with talk. What would you do now, tell me?"

"I'd put in a stick of dynamite and light it. You'd see how gracefully the Ratter would get out!"

"And if he doesn't get out?"

"That wouldn't be any loss either."

Justito the mayor, nevertheless, two days before, in the square, had bumped into señora Clo, who ran the tobacco shop, and she had called him aside. "Justito," she said to him. "Is it true that you and Fito are trying to throw the Ratter out of his cave? What harm is he doing?"

"The thing is, señora Clo, one day it'll fall in and the town will have an unfortunate accident."

She said, "Fix it up for him; that's easy."

The welt on the forehead of Justito the mayor reddened visibly.

"Really, it isn't that, señora Clo. Really it's because of

93

the tourists, you know. The tourists come and then go back saying that we Spaniards live in caves. What do you think of that?"

"Tourists, tourists . . . Let them say what they please! Don't they walk around showing off their bare legs and nobody says anything to them?"

As if this weren't enough, José Luis the bailiff pointed out clearly one day to Justito the impossibility of just going out and blowing up the Ratter's cave. José Luis, after a prolonged conference with the judge at Torrecillórigo, came to the conclusion that the Ratter, without spending a single peseta, was the owner of his cave.

"Owner?" said Justito all perplexed. "Can you kindly tell me to whom he paid two *reales* for it?"

José Luis assumed an all-knowing look: "Money!" he said. "In the eyes of the law, money's not the only thing that counts, Justo, let's not push it. Time counts too."

"Time?"

"Look. Pay attention now, you have something for a while and a day. With nothing but time going by you become the owner of it. That's the way it is."

Justito frowned and the welt palpitated like a living thing: "Even though you've stolen it?"

"Even though you've stolen it."

"We've had it then," said Justito, disconsolate.

Starting with the lawsuit over the cave, Columba began to look askance at Nini as at her most direct and bitterest enemy. But even so, Nini, the little boy, seemed not to know how she felt, and it never crossed his mind that a day might come when he might have to make such a bold decision as to pour a can of gasoline into Justito's well. Nevertheless, one thing followed another, and when on San Bernardino de Sena's day, Columba sent a message to Nini, as every year, to take the chicks from the hen, the boy came trustingly, plucked the feathers from the breast of the capon, applied a handful of nettles to him, and then set him in the box on top of the worried chicks to calm down. The hen, meanwhile, was stupidly watching him through the bars of

94

her pen as if none of it had anything to do with her. But as the boy finished, Columba, instead of giving him the bread and chocolate as she usually did, just stood there watching him with the same stupid expression as the hen. Columba would say sometimes that Nini's face wore a cold expression from Virgin's day in July to Assumption day in August, when the dog days were at their worst. Malvino explained that that happens to everybody who thinks a lot, because while the brain is working, the head heats up and the face gets cold, since the body calories are countable and if you put them in one place, you have to take them from another. When Big Wagger was present, he agreed with the tavernkeeper and told them that when don Eustacio de la Piedra, who was a scholar, felt his father's vertebrae, his face too wore a cold expression. But Nini, now, under Columba's impassive stare, could only manage to say, "Well, it's ready."

Then she seemed to wake up; she put her hand on the boy's shoulder and said, "Nini, will you kindly tell me why you two don't get out of the cave?"

"No," the boy said sullenly.

"You're not getting out or you're not going to tell me?"

"Both."

"Both! Both!" Columba shook him and her angry voice kept gradually rising in pitch. "One day rheumatism will eat your bones because you live underground and then you won't be able to open your mouth or move a foot."

Nini remained calm. "But look at rabbits," he said calmly.

Columba, then, lost control of herself, raised her hand, and gave the boy two solid cuffs. Afterward, as if she were the one offended, she raised her two hands to her cheeks and began to cry, her body racked with wild sobbing.

That same night, Nini stole a can of gasoline from the Rich Man's shed and emptied it in Justito's well. The next morning, as usual, Columba started the day with a glass of water, and as she finished, she smacked her tongue: "This water has a funny taste," she said.

"For God's sake . . ." said Justito patiently.

"I tell you it has a funny taste," insisted Columba.

And when he put his nose in the bucket, Justito's hands shook visibly: "You know you're right? This water smells like gasoline."

He struck a match and the liquid in the bucket burned furiously. Justito began to beat his fists against his chest and laugh boisterously. Very excited, he went to get his bicycle and told Columba with much waving of arms: "Not a word about this, hear? There's petroleum down here. I'm going to tell the Chief. This is more important than the caves. But until the Chief gets here, not a word, you hear?"

In the afternoon the Chief arrived in his little car. The sun still had not set but it was that time of day when you could already hear the stone curlews on the slope of Merino Hill and the crickets were deafening with their frantic song from the fields.

Justito, with trembling hands, made the demonstration, and the Chief, seeing the bucket burn, felt a paralyzing cold run through him—which paradoxically made his bald head sweat torrents. "Well, well . . . ," he said at last with a nervous wink of complicity, "an expert has to see this. This may be a real find. Not even I can foresee the possibilities. I'll be back tomorrow. Until then, let's keep it very quiet."

By nightfall, the entire town was stationed before Justito's house. Rosalino the foreman took the floor and said they had news that the governor had been there incognito and that Antoliano and Big Wagger had seen the car and that something important must be happening in the town and that Justo being their mayor it was his duty to tell them all about it.

At the end of his speech, the intense clamor of the crickets descended from the hills like a suffocating aroma and flooded everything and Justo the mayor hesitated and, finally, said, "It's nothing. Nothing's happened, I tell you."

But señora Librada, Sabina's mother, Pruden's wife, yelled out with her stentorian high voice, "Come on Justito, don't make us twist your arm."

96

And Dominica, Antoliano's wife, said, "That's not nice, Justo."

And Justo turned to her. "What's not nice, Dominica?"

And Dominica said, "Making us twist your arm."

Then Justito raised his hands to quiet them and said, "All right." And with affected restraint he went over to the well, took out a small bucket of water and set it afire. The flames ascended spiraling toward the high dark heavens and Justito from the depths of his chest spoke in his official mayor's voice. "Friends! From Donalcio Hill to the Nipple of Torrecillórigo there's a sea of petroleum down under here. The Chief said so. Tomorrow we'll all be rich. Now, I just ask one favor of you all: let's stay calm and keep it quiet."

A great cry of enthusiasm chorused his words. Men and women hugged one another, dirty berets flew through the air, and Pruden pulled off his worn brown corduroy jacket and jumped up and down on it like a madman. From time to time he got off it and said, "Step on it, Dominica. Down there there's a fortune. We've got to keep it warm." And Mamés the mute drooling, turned to the mayor as though he were going to make a speech, but he only said, "Hu!" and from the corner of his mouth a bit of yellowish foam slipped out. And he repeated, "Hu!" Then Sabina, beside herself, shouted, "The mute has said something! The mute has said something!" And Virgilio, riding on Malvino's shoulders, screamed, "Frutos, the skyrockets!" And Frutos the notary was back from the town hall in a flash and the skyrockets ripped the dark shadows of the sky with their luminous trails and exploded on high with short abortive bangs. Señora Clo went stumbling toward Sabina, making her way through the crowd, but on seeing Virgilio on Malvino's shoulders she screamed at him, "Get down from there, Virgilio. You're going to fall!" Then she asked Sabina, "Sabina, is it true that the mute said something?" And Sabina said, "He said, 'Hurrah!' Everybody heard him." Doña Resu, behind her, crossed herself. Only Guadalupe

97

and his men seemed to be out of place in that noisy confusion, standing in a tight group, their heads hanging. Their boss finally pushed his way through the mob and faced Justito. He said darkly, "And us, Justito? What are we going to get out of all this?"

The mayor was exultant. He said to him, "We'll give you all a share, obviously. There's enough petroleum here for everybody. You can bring your wives and children and come live here with us."

Nobody in town slept that night, and the next morning, as soon as the governor arrived with two serious and enigmatic men in the big car, the excited and sleepy multitude gathered around him. But when Justito lit a match and put it to the little bucket and the match went out, there was a murmur of disappointment. Justito grew pale but he persisted three more times with the same result, until finally the governor invited him to go into the house with the bucket and the two serious and enigmatic men. When they came out, the crowd surrounded them expectantly and the governor, with Justito pushing on his behind, climbed up clumsily on the rim of the well. With a strained voice he said, "Farmers, you have been the victims of a cruel joke. There is no petroleum here. But don't lose heart on that account. You have petroleum in the hooves of your horses and in the shares of your plows. Keep working and with your efforts you'll raise your standard of living and contribute to the greatness of Spain. Let's give a cheer for agriculture!"

There was no applause. When he got down from the top of the well the governor nervously wiped a very white handkerchief over his shiny bald pate, gave Justito a gentle friendly pat on the back, and murmured, "I'm sorry." Then he raised his voice and said, "I'm really sorry." And turning to the serious and enigmatic gentlemen, he said, pointing to the automobile, "Whenever you're ready." A uniformed chauffeur opened the door for them; they got in and the big car disappeared down the road in a cloud of dust.

13

As he stepped out of the shadow into the light, blinded by the first rays of the rising sun, the Old Ratter blinked. From the interior of the cave, against the light, he seemed chubbier and bigger than he really was: standing stock still with his beret pulled down to his ears he looked like a statue. His arms hung down at his sides, and his hands, with their fingers all the same length as though cut by a paper cutter, easily reached his knees. After a few seconds he opened his eyes and looked out over the vast fields of wheat burning with poppies. The repetitive song of the crickets now had an invigorating rhythm like some energy used for the first time. The Ratter's eyes ever so slowly looked up to the distant gray hilltops that seemed like ships with their naked keels to the sun; then his gaze slid down the bare slopes until it stopped at the little plank bridge that joined the cave with the town.

"We'll have to go down," he said with an almost inaudible grunt.

Nini went up to him, followed by the dogs, and stopped at his side. His eyes were still sleepy, but the big toe of his right foot mechanically rubbed against the one-eyed bitch's fur and Fa stood motionless, enjoying it, while Loy, the pup, played madly around her.

"It may be worse," said the boy. "We'll spoil the nests and we won't get anywhere."

The man blew his nose, one nostril after the other, and

then wiped it with the back of his hand. He said, "We've got to eat something."

Since the rats had begun to get scarce, the Old Ratter had become more and more tight-lipped. The dirty beret pulled down to his ears outlined the form of his skull and the boy wondered frequently what possibly might be going on under it. In previous years, about this season, after the outdoor meal of Santa Elena and San Casto's day, the Ratter had always saved enough to get through the summer, but this last year had been a bad one and now that the closed season was on them, hunger rose up before them like a black ghost.

The boy insisted, "On San Vito's day crayfish open. Maybe it'll be a good year."

The Old Ratter sighed deeply and said nothing. He had raised his eyes again and fixed them on the bare gray hilltops that enclosed the horizon. Nini added, "By summer, we'll go up to the woods and take the bark off the oaks. Marcelino the tanner pays well. It's probably better to wait."

The Ratter didn't answer. He whistled softly and Loy the pup obeyed the whistle. Then the Ratter squatted down and said with a smile, "This one can see," and began to pet him and Loy growled with playful rage and pretended to bite his rough hands.

The days with nothing to do were long, and usually the Ratter filled them by cleaning up the cave, or training the pup down by the river or speaking in monosyllables, at sunset, on the stone bench by Antoliano's door or at Malvino's tavern. Some nights, before going to bed, everybody went together to the stable to see Little Wagger milk the cows. And they would say to him, "Today without talking to them, Wag." And when the Little Wagger was finishing, they'd say to themselves, "She gave less milk, you know." And the next day they would say to him, "Speak to the cow while you're milking her, Wag." And then the Little Wagger would start a mellifluous monologue and he would get a bucket more and they would nudge one another with their elbows and would say with approving gestures, "What do you think of that? That's pretty neat."

Sometimes while they smoked lazily in the stable or on the stone bench Antoliano had at his shop the conversation came back again to the ratter from Torrecillórigo, and Antoliano would say, "Knock his block off, Ratter. What do you think your hands are for?" Then the Old Ratter would tremble and sputter, "Just let me set my eyes on him." And Rosalino would say, "Nobody could get away with that with me." And if the gathering was at the tavern, Malvino would go up to the Old Ratter and say to him, "Ratter, if a poor man enters a rich man's house, obviously he's a thief, isn't he?"

"A thief," agreed the Ratter.

"But if a rich man enters a poor man's house, what is he?"

"What is he?" the Old Ratter repeated stupidly.

"A rat!"

The Ratter stubbornly denied this, shaking his head.

"No," he said finally. "Rats are good."

Malvino persisted.

"And I say, Ratter: Is money the only thing you can steal?"

The Old Ratter's eyes got more and more clouded.

"That's right," he would say.

On Santa Elena and San Casto's day, there were no rats for anyone, and the party to celebrate the last hunting day turned out to be dismal and sad. The Ratter pulled out of his sack, one after the other, about five catches.

"There are no more," he said finally.

Pruden began to laugh ill-humoredly. "For this trip," he said, "you didn't need bags."

The Ratter eyed the group gloomily and repeated, "There aren't any more rats. He's stealing them from me."

Malvino went up to him and said in anger, "And consider yourself lucky, man, because by next year there won't even be one left for you to tell about."

The forearms of the Old Ratter bulged with muscles as he

hooked his fingers, and he said suddenly in a hoarse voice, "If I catch him, I'll kill him."

Nini tried to quiet him down.

"If there aren't any rats, there'll be crayfish. Forget it."

The Ratter did not answer, and when night came, he went up to the cave and lit his lantern and sat silent at the entrance. The crickets were chirping themselves hoarse down below in the fields, and the mosquitoes and the moths were swirling in concentric circles around the flame. From time to time, there swept over their heads a gust like the crackling of very dry wood. The boy raised his eyes, and the dogs growled.

"The goatsucker," Nini said by way of explanation.

But the Ratter didn't hear him. On the following day Nini, as every morning, tried hard to find a solution. At dawn he left the cave and passed the day hunting lizards, collecting manzanilla, or cutting milkweed for the rabbits. Some days, even, he got as far as the summits of the most forbidding hills above the cave to gather wild almonds. But all that, put together, didn't amount to much. Although their flesh was tender and tasty, the lizards really didn't have much meat to eat; the manzanilla don Cristino, the pharmacist of Torrecillórigo, bought for three pesetas the kilo, and as for the milkweed señora Clo, Pruden, or Antoliano bought them from him at a *real* per armful just to do him a favor. Once Nini tried to increase his clientele, but the townspeople were too stingy.

"A *real* for an armful? But, my boy, there are plenty of milkweeds right in the ditch by the side of the road."

One late afternoon, the eve of San Restituto's day, Nini again came upon the young man from Torrecillórigo in the river bottom. The boy tried to avoid him, but the young man came over to him smiling, beating the palm of his hand with the back side of his iron bar. Fa sniffed the tail of his dog among the reeds. The young man said, "What's your name, kid?"

"Nini."

"Just Nini?"

"Nini. What's yours?"

"Luis."

"Luis? That's a funny name."

"You think Luis is a funny name?"

"In my town nobody has that name."

The young man burst out laughing and his dazzling white teeth sparkled in his dark face.

"Don't you suppose the names in your town are funny?"

Nini shrugged his shoulders, and sat down on the riverbank. The young man went over to the river bottom, where the dog was hunting through the brush, and said in a matter-of-fact tone, "Get him, go get him."

Then he came back where the boy was and sat down beside him, took out his tobacco pouch and packet, and rolled a cigarette. As he lit it with his flint lighter he looked at him, and in the sun, his eyes were striated like a cat's. Nini said to him, "You shouldn't hunt any more."

"So?"

"If you destroy the nests, you'll finish off the rats."

The young man set his iron bar on end and balanced it for a few seconds on his index finger. Then he suddenly withdrew his hand and caught it in the air as though catching a fly. He began to laugh.

"Even if that's so, kid," he said, "who's going to cry over them?"

The sun was sinking behind the hills and the crickets were deafening all around. Now and then, among the rushes very close, you could hear the mating call of a quail.

"Don't you like to hunt?" Nini inquired.

"Look, it's a way to pass the time. But I also like to take a walk with a girl."

When the sun set, Nini would return from his expeditions and join the Old Ratter on the stone bench at Antoliano's door, or in the stables of the Rich Man, or at Malvino's tavern. In any case, the attitude of the Ratter didn't change: there he sat mute, his eyes evasive, forearms resting on his thighs, motionless as though lying in wait for something. If by chance the group got together at the stables, the Ratter, leaning back on the manger, would watch Little Wagger closely and, when he finished milking, would shake his head in a vague affirmative way and murmur, "That's neat, that is." And his neighbor, whether it were Pruden, Virgilio, Big Wagger, or Antoliano would nudge him with his elbow and say to him, "What do you think of that, Ratter?" And he would repeat, "That's neat, that is."

On Santa Petronila and Santa Angela de Merici's day, the Eleventh Commandment spoke to the Old Ratter once again.

"Have you thought about it, Ratter?" she said to him as soon as she saw him.

"Nini is mine," the Ratter said sullenly.

"Listen," added the Eleventh Commandment, "I'm not trying to take Nini away from you, just make a man of him. Doña Resu only wants the boy to make a future for himself. That way, when the day comes, people will call him 'Mister' and he'll earn a lot of money and buy himself an automobile and he'll be able to drive you through town. Wouldn't you like that, Ratter, drive through town in an automobile?"

"No," the Old Ratter said drily.

"All right. But surely you'd like to leave the cave someday and build a house of your own with a place to sit and sun and a well-stocked larder on Donalcio Hill—God bless him—wouldn't you?"

"No," said the Ratter. "The cave is mine."

Doña Resu raised both hands to her head and held it tight as though she were afraid it might fly away.

"All right," she repeated. "It's apparent that the only thing that amuses you, Ratter, is to get my goat. But you must understand that if he tries, Nini could learn a lot of things —as much as an engineer. Do you realize that?"

The Ratter scratched himself roughly under his beret: "They know about things?" he asked.

"Goodness me! Any problem you give an engineer, he'll solve it in five minutes."

The Ratter stopped scratching himself and quickly raised his head.

"What about the pines?" he said suddenly.

"The pines? Look, Ratter, no man, however intelligent he may be, can do anything against the will of the Lord. The Lord willed that the hillsides of Castille should be bare, and against that all the strength of mankind is of no avail. Do you realize that?"

The Ratter nodded his agreement. Doña Resu's spirits seemed to rise. She softened her voice and continued, "Your boy is intelligent, Ratter, but it's just like a field without seed. The boy could go to the school at Torrecillórigo and when the day comes we could make arrangements for him to study a profession. Ratter, all you have to do is to tell me yes or no. If you say yes, I'll take the boy—"

"Nini is mine," said the Ratter sulkily.

Doña Resu's voice went sharp.

"All right, Ratter, you keep him. I hope you don't regret this, come tomorrow."

As evening came, when the first lights went on in town and the swifts were settling down for the night, twittering excitedly under the eaves of the belfry, doña Resu went to the town hall.

"These people," she said peevishly to Justito, "would kill to better their condition, but if you offer them an opportunity on a silver platter, they'd kill you so they wouldn't be forced to accept it; do you realize that, Justo?"

Justito the mayor tapped his forehead three times with his finger and said, "The Ratter has something missing up here. If he doesn't bray, it's because he never learned."

José Luis put in, "Why don't we give him a test?"

"A test?" said doña Resu.

"Look. Those questions they ask people. If there's a doctor who will say that he's got a screw loose or that he's mentally retarded they'll lock him up and that's the end of it."

Justito's face lit up.

"Like with Walker?" he asked.

"Just the same."

Two months back, when he was returning one Sunday from Torrecillórigo, Agapito—Walker—ran over a child with his bicycle, and in order to make a legal decision on his responsibility he was sent to the capital for questioning; and the doctors arrived at the conclusion that Walker's intelligence was that of an eight-year-old child. Agapito was very amused by the experiment and from that moment became a bit more talkative; at every opportunity, he would use the questions as riddles at the bar. "Shall I give you a test?" he would say. Other times he would boast about his performance: "The doctor said to me, 'If in railroad accidents the last car is the one that has the most people killed and hurt, what would you do to solve the problem?' And I said to him, 'If that's all it is, doctor, it's pretty simple: take the last car off.' And the people in the capital think us townsfolk are stupid."

"If the Chief authorizes it, a test could be the solution," said Justito.

Doña Resu lowered her eyes and said, "Well, after all, if we take all this trouble, it's for his own good. The Ratter has the mind of a child and we won't get anywhere treating him like a man."

14

The Sunday after Easter a terrible tragedy almost happened in the town. A little before the ceremonies started, the bell clapper hit Antoliano in the back of the neck and Mamertito, Pruden's boy, slipped off the tower with the rope tied around his waist. Fortunately Antoliano recovered in time and stamped his foot on the rope, and Mamertito hung there swinging back and forth in space with his sky-blue tunic pulled up under his armpits and his little white plastic wings broken by the violent jerk.

From the square, Nini watched the whole affair nervously, since just two years before he had been the one who played Mamertito's part; but Matías Celemín, the Weasel, despite the fact that the evening before his bitch greyhound had died, let out a guffaw and said, "The little rascal looks like a little bustard that's had his wings clipped." That was the end of the incident, however, and doña Resu, the Eleventh Commandment, ordered Antoliano to hoist the child back up since the Extremadurans weren't there yet and the ceremonies couldn't start.

It had cost doña Resu, the Eleventh Commandment, a real effort to compromise with the conditions set by Guadalupe, the boss, but the disappointment aroused in the townsfolk by the petroleum business had not entirely dissipated, and as Rosalino the foreman told her, "This year they had no desire to play the clown." Only after much effort had doña Resu managed to recruit six Apostles, but Guadalupe, the boss, had shown himself to be uncompromising in this respect: "All of us, or none of us, doña Resu, that's the way it is. We Extremadurans are like that."

And rather than let the Pascuilla ceremony suffer, doña Resu authorized the twelve Extremadurans to wear the much-patched smocks of the Apostles.

Over the dusty square hung a swollen sticky sun, and way up high, up where the noise of the crowd couldn't reach, three black vultures were lazily planing around. Nini didn't know where those birds lived, but all that was needed was the body of a cat or a lamb in the fallow fields for them to come flying in over the hilltops. Beneath them flocks of swifts darted in and out of the bays in the tower, accompanying their movements with a deafening chatter.

Finally, around the corner of the church, the Extremadurans appeared. Nini saw them approaching with their heavy gait, their rough corduroy pants, and their coarse boots, muddied with clay, peeping out from under their multicolored tunics. The almost hairless wigs, clumsily set on their heads, spilled down over their shoulders, and yet the group did present a convincing biblical appearance that was heightened by the background of adobe houses and the brushwood fences of the barnyards.

The people opened up a path for them and the Extremadurans filed silently along it with their heads bowed, and when they reached the steps of the church, they suddenly burst apart like gunshot among the crowd and began to open doors, and jump over garden walls and lift stones, in a feverish search, until doña Resu, gotten up in the blue tunic and the white veil of the Virgin, made an imperceptible signal to Antoliano; and Mamertito began to descend, slowly now, from the top of the tower, swinging over the crowd, his wings still crumpled, but full of unctuous transcendency.

Upon spying the Angel, the Virgin, the Apostles, and the people prostrated themselves, overcome with amazement, and a heavy silence ensued; and above the hysterical shrill-

ing of the swifts the voice of Mamertito rose sweetly saying, "Do not look for him. For Jesus, called the Nazarene,
has come to life again."

Mamertito floated for a few instants longer above the
square, while the faithful crossed themselves and Antoliano,
bit by bit, hauled in on the rope. As soon as the Angel disappeared behind the bay of the tower, doña Resu straightened up painfully and said, "We praise you, Christ, and
bless you . . ."

And the devout congregation chorused, ". . . who
through your holy cross redeemed the world."

With that they all went into the church and got down on
their knees, while upstairs in the choir, Frutos the notary
released a dove from Justo's dovecote. The bird, confused,
flew around over the crowd for a few minutes, knocking
itself several times against the windowpanes, and finally
went and alighted on Simeona's right shoulder. Then the
Eleventh Commandment turned around to the townsfolk
from the steps of the altar and said pompously to Sime, "My
daughter, the Spirit has descended upon you."

Sime wiggled her shoulder unobtrusively, trying to scare
the dove off, but seeing it was futile, she resigned herself
and began to swallow hard, making odd little sounds as if
she were choking to death, and in the end she let herself
be led by doña Resu to the torch stand and once there,
everybody filed past in front of her and some kissed her
hands, and others genuflected and the more timid sketched
surreptitiously over their suntanned faces something that
could have been a furtive sign of the cross. When they finished paying their respects, Sime, guarded by the Apostles
and preceded by the Virgin and the Angel of Good News,
who marked the time with a flute and timbrel, paraded
through the streets of the town, as night fell gently over
the hills.

When the procession started, Nini ran off to see Centenarian, who now was hardly more than a bundle of bones
after so many enemas:

"Señor Rufo," he said panting, "the dove alighted on Sime this afternoon."

The old man sighed, lifted with difficulty a finger toward the roof and said, "The vultures are up there already. I felt they were there this morning."

"I saw them," said the boy. "There were three of them and they were flying above the tower. They're after Weasel's bitch greyhound."

Centenarian shook his head in a firm negative. Finally he said with great effort, pointing to his left shoulder, "They're going to land here."

And indeed, on the following afternoon, which was San Francisco Caracciolo's day, Centenarian passed away. Sime lay the corpse on the floor in the entrance hall, face up, on a strip of burlap, and took the rag off his face so the bone shone brightly in the light of the candles. Dressed in mourning, the townspeople gathered silently around him. When Nini came in, Sime said to him, "There he is. Finally the two of us can rest."

But Old Man Rufo didn't seem to be resting, with his one eye and his mouth pathetically open. Nor did Sime seem to be resting either, because she kept swallowing with those little choking sounds, like the night before when the Spirit descended upon her. But to each person who came she repeated the same story. Then a big fly, which had settled for ten minutes on Centenarian's fleshless face, buzzed over the assembly, and everybody except Sime and the boy began to wave his arms to shoo it off. The big fly returned to the corpse, which was doubtless the most dispassionate of all, but each time it took to the air, the men and the women tried to hide their efforts to keep it away, and so it was that they made a whispering noise like the blades of a fan. Half an hour later Antoliano appeared with the pine box still smelling of pitch, and Sime asked them to lend a hand, but they all held back, until between her, Nini, and Antoliano, they managed to get him into it. Since Antoliano, to save wood, had taken exact measurements, Old Man Rufo lay there with his head shoved down into his shoulders as if he were humpbacked or were just saying that not a thing in this world was any longer of any interest to him.

In midafternoon, don Ciro the priest arrived with Mamertito, and sprinkled the corpse with his hyssop and knelt at the feet and said in anguished tones, "Bend, O Lord, your ear to our prayers with which we implore your mercy so that you will put in the place of light and peace the soul of your servant Rufo, whom you have called upon to leave this world. For our Lord Jesus Christ. . . ."

And Mamertito said, "Amen."

And at that moment the big fly took off from the corpse and flew straight to the tip of don Ciro's nose, but don Ciro, with his eyes lowered, his hands crossed gently over his cassock, seemed to be in ecstasy and didn't notice. And everybody there nudged one another and murmured, "The cancer will eat away his nose." But don Ciro paid no attention, until with no warning he sneezed noisily and the big fly, startled, sought refuge once again upon the corpse.

When the prayers were finished, señora Clo came forward with the moth-eaten book and Sime said, "What's this for? It belonged to the old man."

On the first page it said, "SERMONS FOR THE MOST CLASSIC MYSTERIES OF THE FEAST DAYS OF JESUS CHRIST AND THE MOST HOLY MARY. THE AUTHOR IS THE GRADUATE IN SACRED CANON LAW DON JOAQUIN ANTONIO DE EGULETA PRESBYTER AND CHAPLAIN MAJOR OF THE CHURCH OF SAN IGNATIUS OF LOYOLA IN THIS CAPITAL. VOLUME III. MADRID MDCCXCVI. WITH THE NECESSARY PERMITS."

Sime raised her eyes and again asked, "What's this for? It was his book."

"Look," said señora Clo.

And she opened it in the middle and there appeared a folded sheet of paper containing a five-peseta note. And on the paper clumsily scrawled out it said, *Sayvins to by me falls teeth.* And on the next page there was another five-peseta bill, and another on the next, and so on up to twenty-five. Señora Clo wet her thumb, counted the money expertly, bill by bill, and handed it over to Simeona.

"Take it," she said to her, "you didn't expect it, but it's yours. The false teeth can't do the old man any good now."

On the following day, San Bonifacio and San Doroteo, when the young men hoisted the bier, the small talk in town revolved around señora Clo's discovery, but more surprising still than the bills was the fact that Centenarian should have had a book in his house. And Malvino said with evident skepticism: "So could he read, or did he forget how? I say anyone who owns a book must be able to read."

On the way to the church, the young men set the bier down to rest three times, and each time don Ciro led the suitable prayers and responses, while Sime became more and more impatient sitting on her little wagon next to Nini; and Duke, the dog, tied to the back with a rope like a noose, whined discordantly. Once at the church, hardly had the men deposited the coffin in the wagon than Sime prodded the donkey, and he took off at top speed to the amazement of all present. Sime's hair was all unkempt, her eyes shining, her jaw clenched, but until they reached the top of the rise, she didn't open her mouth. Then she said to Nini, "You, what do you think you're doing here, hmmm?"

The boy looked at her seriously, "I just want to be with the old man," he said.

Then they were at the cemetery, and between the two of them they dragged the coffin to the hole in the ground and the girl began to shovel in the dirt on top of it with considerable spirit. The box sounded hollow and Sime's eyes started to get damper and damper, until Nini confronted her, "Sime, is something wrong?"

She rubbed the back of her hand across her forehead. Then she said, almost furiously, "Can't you see the dust I'm raising?"

When they left, next to the ironwork gate, Loy sniffed at Duke's tail. An ineffable peace was spreading over the hilltops. Sime pointed to Loy with her shovel, "He doesn't even know it's his father: what a world!"

On the way back, the donkey kept up an indecorous trot that speeded up as he descended the hill. But Sime drove the wagon by the path along Donalcio Hill and entered the town by the church instead of coming in by the Rich Man's barn. Nini said to her, "Sime, aren't you going home?"

"No," said Sime.

And before the door of the Eleventh Commandment she stopped the little wagon, got down, and knocked twice lightly with the knocker. Doña Resu, opening the door, looked as though she had a stomach ache.

"Sime. My word. The Eleventh: *Thou shalt not disturb people.*"

Nini expected that Sime would give some acid reply, but to his surprise the girl bowed her head and humbly said in a whisper, "Excuse me, doña Resu; if you're not busy, go with me to the church. I want to offer myself."

The Eleventh Commandment crossed herself, then stood away from the door and said, "Praise be to God. Come in, child. The Lord has called you."

15

On the day of Our Lady of the Light the sheepbane sprouted on the meadow and Nini hustled to pass the news on to Big Wagger so he could move his sheep, since, as he knew from Centenarian, the sheep that eats sheepbane develops a worm in its liver and becomes useless. That same afternoon Pruden told the boy that moles were digging up his garden and keeping the Swiss chard and potatoes from growing. In the late afternoon Nini came down the river bottom and for an hour was busy making little holes in the ground to connect the tunnels. Nini knew, from Grandpa Román, that if there's a draft in the tunnels the moles catch cold and at dawn come out of their lairs to cover them up.

Nini was working half-heartedly, as though at play, guided in his chore by the little heaps of spongy earth that were all around him. Fa, who had suddenly grown old, watched him work as she lay panting in the sparse shadow of some reeds, while Loy, the cinnamon pup, pranced about on the gravel chasing green lizards.

On the following day, San Erasmo and Santa Blandina, the boy went down again to the garden before sunup. The haze clouded the shape of the hills, making them seem more distant, and on the plants the dew was condensing. Next to the bank a quail flew up noisily while the crickets and the frogs, confusedly and noisily announcing the arrival of a new day, grew more and more quiet as the boy approached. Reaching the garden, Nini posted himself in a corner near the stream; and hardly had ten minutes gone by before a quiet sound, like that of rabbits in their hole, told him the mole had come out. The creature moved clumsily, halting frequently, and after a last pause, went to one of the holes made by the boy and began to pile up dirt, pushing it with his nose over the opening. Loy, the pup, upon spying it crouched down on his forepaws and barked furiously, then pranced awkwardly in feigned attack; but the boy pulled him aside, scolding him, and picked up the mole carefully and put him in the basket. In less than an hour, he caught three more moles and as the red splendor of the sun announced itself over the hilltops and spread out the first shadows, Nini straightened up, stretched his little arms lazily, and said to the dogs, "Off we go." At the foot of Red Hill, José Luis the bailiff was spreading manure on the fallow field, and a little lower down, on the other bank of the river, Antoliano was patiently tying up the escarole and the lettuce so they would blanch. From town came the tinkling of the flock and the ill-humored and sleepy voices of the Extremadurans in the Rich Man's yard.

Sixty feet downstream, as Nini reached the reeds, the partridge eagle unexpectedly flew up. It was an unlikely thing for the eagle to spend the night in the rushes and it did not take long for Nini to find the nest, roughly constructed upon a thorn tree bush with a few sticks interlaced covered over with the skin of a young hare. Two eaglets, one bigger than the other, focused their round distrusting eyes upon him, raising their curved beaks in threat. The boy smiled, pulled up a rush, and stood awhile provoking them, poking them until he made them desperate. Way up in the blue of the sky, the mother eagle flew in big circles over his head.

Nini didn't say a word about his discovery, but every evening he would go down into the rushes to observe the progress of the eaglets, and the activities of their mother, who from time to time returned to the nest clutching in her rapacious talons a lizard, a rat, or a partridge. On each return, the eagle, perched on the top of the thorn tree, scrutinized the surroundings with majestic arrogance before tearing the hide off her prey to give it to her little ones. Hidden among the rushes, the boy watched her movements, the frantic greed of the little eagles devouring the catch, the proud satisfaction of the mother eagle before soaring back up into the blue. And so the little eagles started to sprout their feathers and grow, until one afternoon Nini discovered that the smaller one had disappeared from the nest and that the big one had been tied with a bit of wire to a branch of the thorn tree. While he hurriedly cut the bond, he thought of Matías Celemín, the Weasel, and then he had no thought for anything because the eagle was plummeting straight down at him from an altitude of a thousand feet and Fa and Loy were barking as they looked up while continuing to back away. The eagle in its descent barely grazed the nest, seized the liberated baby in its talons and zoomed up again with it and flew off toward the woods.

Two days later, on the Triumph of Saint Paul day, the north wind blew in and the weather cooled. The sunsets were colder and the crickets and quail subdued their evening concerts. On the following day, San Medardo, the wind slackened; and in the evening the ceiling lifted and over the town there hung a quiet and transparent atmosphere. When night fell, the moon came up, a white and distant moon that rose gradually over the hilltops. As the Ratter and Nini arrived at the tavern, Chuco, Malvino's dog, was barking angrily at the moon from the barnyard and his barking echoed sharply in the crystal night. Malvino was worried. He said, "What ails that animal tonight?"

Little by little, as though by mutual agreement, all the men from the town came to the tavern. One by one they entered, their black berets pulled down to their ears, and before sitting down on the benches they looked around fearfully and suspiciously. One heard, from time to time, only the noise of a glass on the table or an angry curse. The air was thickening with smoke and when Pruden appeared in the doorway, twenty tanned faces turned toward him

116

anxiously. Pruden hesitated on the threshold. He looked very pale and unsteady. He said, "The stars are shining pretty bright. Do you think there's a black frost on the way?"

He was answered by silence and, in the background, by the insistent and methodical barking of Chuco in the barnyard. Pruden looked around before he sat down; behind him he heard Rosalino the foreman curse, and as he turned Rosalino said to him, "If I were God, I'd let you do what you damn well pleased with the weather, just so as not to have to listen to you."

After Rosalino's angry remark the silence grew thicker and more dramatic. José Luis the bailiff stirred nervously before he said, "Malvino, couldn't you make that dog shut up?"

The tavernkeeper went out and from inside they heard the kick and the painful howling of the animal as it ran away. In the big room inside the tension seemed to increase when Malvino came back. Guadalupe the boss, after a bit, said as though through a fog, "When did it ever freeze on San Medardo's day?"

The forty eyes now converged upon him, and to get rid of his nervousness Guadalupe emptied his glass in one gulp. Malvino came over to him with the bottle and filled the glass without the other's asking. Then he said, bottle in hand, determined to face the inevitable squarely: "Not that. It's about twenty years now since the freeze on Santa Oliva's day, you remember? The grain was grown to stalks and dry and in less than a couple of hours the damned frost cleaned it out."

The evil spell was suddenly broken.

"It probably wasn't more than twenty or thirty bushels, what we got in the whole town," added Antoliano.

Justito the mayor, from the corner table, shouted, "That happens only once. We're not going to see anything like that again."

Antoliano was vigorously waving his hamlike hands at

117

the next table, explaining the disaster to Virgilio, señora
Clo's husband.

"The wheat spikes looked like they were scorched, you
know? Just as if a fire had passed over them. Just as if. All
burned."

The tavernkeeper was filling up the glasses, and their
tongues, at first sluggish, were now getting into action. You
would have thought that with that hot exchange of words
they were hoping to conjure away the danger of frost. Suddenly, dominating the conversation, they could hear
Chuco's woeful howling in the yard again.

Nini said, "That dog's barking as though someone had
died."

No one answered him and Chuco's howls became more
and more mournful, passing from table to table like a
cramp. Malvino went out into the yard. His curses were
mingled with the plaintive squealing of the dog and the
noise of the slamming door as Weasel came in. Matías
Celemín, breathing hard as though he'd come a long way,
said, "It's coming down good. The ruts are as stiff as in
January. Out in the vegetable gardens there isn't a single
plant standing up. Why are we being punished like this?"

All around one could hear the sound of quiet cursing.
Above it resounded Pruden's voice, excited, vibrant, *Me
cago en mi madre!* he screamed. "Is this living? You work
eleven months like a dog, and then, in one night . . ." He
turned toward Nini. His feverish glance settled on the boy,
expectant, hungry. "Nini, kid," he added, "isn't there some
way out of this?"

"That depends," said the little boy, seriously.

"That depends, that depends . . . depends on what?"

"The wind," answered the boy.

The silence was rigid and tense. The looks of the men
converged now on Nini like the October crows on the crops.
Pruden repeated, "The wind?"

"If the north wind comes back with the dawn, it'll blow

118

the cold away and the wheat'll be saved. The vegetables, now, that's less likely," the boy said.

Pruden got up and walked between the tables. He acted drunk and laughed like a simpleton. "Did you hear that?" he said. "There's still a way out. Why shouldn't the wind start to blow? Isn't it more unlikely to have a freeze on San Medardo's day—and yet it's freezing? Why shouldn't the wind start to blow?"

Suddenly he stopped laughing; he looked around, hoping to find agreement, but he saw nothing but a cloud of skepticism, an angry resignation down deep in their eyes. Then he sat down again and hid his face in his hands. Behind him, Antoliano said to the Ratter in a low voice, "There aren't any rats, we're losing the harvest—can you tell me what in hell ties us to this damned town?" Little Wagger stuttered: "The la-land," he said. "The land is li-like a wife." Rosalino yelled over from the other side of the room, "Yeah, right, she'll knock it up with the first guy that comes along." Mamés the mute was making faces beside Weasel, the variety of contorted grimaces he made every time he became excited. Matías Celemín suddenly shouted, "Shut up, Mute, simmer down, you're making me sick." Frutos the notary then said, "Suppose Virgilio sings us a song?"

As if that were a signal, the men simultaneously shouted from all the tables, "Come on, Virgilio! Sing us something!" Agapito the Walker began to pound the tabletop, keeping time with the palms of his hands. Justito, who for two hours hadn't stopped drinking from his pitcher, raised his voice above the others, "Hit it, Virgilio. Whatever it is will sound good!" And Virgilio cleared his throat a couple of times and started out with "The Lamplighter" and Agapito and Big Wagger beat time with their hands and shortly Frutos, Guadalupe, Antoliano, and José Luis joined them. Minutes later the tavern was boiling and the handclapping mixed with the excited voices singing old, sad songs off key. Smoke filled the room and Malvino the tavernkeeper passed among the tables ceaselessly filling glasses and pitchers to the brim. Outside, the moon was silently describing its age-old parabola over the hill and the rooftops of the town, and the frost was settling down on the vegetables and the young grain.

Time had ceased to exist and when Sabina, Pruden's wife, burst into the tavern, the men looked at one another with watery eyes in surprise, as though wondering why they were all congregated together there. Pruden rubbed his eyes and his glance caught Sabina's empty look, and then Sabina yelled at him, "Will someone please tell me what's going on with you raising all this racket at five o'clock in the morning? Is that all you can think about, to raise hell like little kids when the frost is carrying off your crops?" She stepped forward two steps and stood face to face with Pruden. "You, Acislo, you can't remember the freeze on Santa Oliva, can you? Well, the one tonight is even worse, just so's you know it. The wheat can't stand the cold and is bending over like lead."

Suddenly there was a pathetic silence. The tavern now seemed like the waiting room of a dying man, where no one could bring himself to face the facts, to find out if death hadn't finally come. A cow mooed plaintively down the street, in the Rich Man's stable, and as if this were the awaited signal, Malvino went to the rough window and opened the shutters with a bang. A diffuse light, wintry and cold, came in through the frosty window panes. Still no one else moved. Only when above the silence the hoarse cockle-doodle-doo of Antoliano's white rooster crowed forth did Rosalino get to his feet and say, "Come on, let's go."

Sabina took Pruden by the arm and said to him, "We'll have nothing left, Acislo, you realize that?"

Outside, over the hilltops, the last stars were being blotted out and a crude whitish light started to spread over the valley. The ruts were like stone, and the earth crunched like nutshells under their feet. The crickets sang timidly, and from the top of Donalcio Hill a male partridge insistently called. The men walked along the road with their heads down and Pruden put his arms around Nini's neck and kept saying, "Will the north wind come, Nini? Do you think the north wind will come?"

Nini didn't answer. He was looking now at the iron grating of the gate and the cross in the little cemetery at the top of the hill and it struck him that that group of dejected men walking out into the vast grain fields were waiting for the coming of some ghost. The wheat stalks were bending over, swaying with their tips loaded with frost, and some were already beginning to turn black. Pruden said desolately, as if the whole weight of the night had suddenly dropped straight on him, "The wind won't get here soon enough."

Down below, in the gardens, the vegetables were drooping, their leaves limp, frost-scorched. The group stopped by the fields facing the Nipple of Torrecillórigo and the men stared at the line of the hills that was getting clearer by the moment. Behind Donalcio Hill the light was brighter. From time to time, someone would bend over Nini and murmur to him, "Do you think it's too late yet, kid, do you?" And Nini replied, "Before the sun comes up, there's still time. It's the sun that burns the wheat." And hope was reborn in their hearts.

But the day kept coming relentlessly closer, lighting the hills, outlining the poverty of the adobe houses, and the sky continued clear, and the air continued still, and the men continued to stare with anguished hunger at the horizon.

It happened all of a sudden. First it was a gentle, subtle puff that caressed the wheat. Then the wind took voice and began to descend roughly off the hills, disheveled, bending the canes, making the grain fields undulate like a sea. Soon it was a gusty roar that shook the countryside with fury, and the wheat stalks began to swing back and forth, shaking off the frost, standing straighter and straighter in the golden light of the dawn. The men, facing the wind, smiled tentatively as though hypnotized, not daring to move a single muscle for fear of interfering with the favorable elements. Rosalino the foreman was the first to get his voice back, and turning to them he yelled, "The wind! Don't you hear the wind? It's the wind!"

And the wind took his words and dragged them as far as the town and then, as though in echo, the bell of the church began to ring merrily and as it rang the entire group seemed to wake up and broke forth in incoherent exclamations and Mamés the mute drooled, and walked all around smiling and saying, "Hu, Hu." And Antoliano and Virgilio hoisted Nini over their heads and shouted, "He said so! Nini said so!"

And Pruden, with Sabina sobbing on his neck, got down on his knees in the field, and again and again rubbed his face with the wheat, its seeds dropping between his fingers, as he laughed madly all the while.

16

The small garden plots next to the river were definitely burned by the black frost. Nevertheless, the men of the town went down stubbornly to their gardens and sowed sorrel, cress, curly escarole, green peas, sweet cicely, leeks, and early carrots. Rosalino the foreman trimmed the vineyard of roots and suckers on the grafts and Nini had the job of clearing the hives of drones and selecting rabbits for breeding. A still clement sun kept the temperature constant and under its rays the grain crops matured, headed up, and dried in a few days. Then the town began to bustle with activity. Every minute of the day men and women were cleaning the threshing floors and readying the tools for the threshing, and at the end of the day one found them disinfecting the granaries to make them ready to receive the grain. Against the sky, which was intensely blue, one day the new storks in the belfry tried their wings, corroborating the proverb of señor Rufo, now dead, "On San Juan's day the storks will fly away."

And yet, every morning the men of the town looked intently toward Northwest Pass, which during the first ten days of the month had stayed calm and clear. Pruden kept saying on every occasion, "What we need now is for it not to rain." Centenarian had been in the habit of remarking with his proverbial forcefulness, "Rain in June brings misfortune." And the men of the valley waited for the sun each morning with the same vehemence with which they waited for rain on Our Lady of Sancho Abarca's or on San Saturio's day. Nevertheless, through the community there spread a premature optimism on the day of Saint Basil the Great. The fact of having saved the grain from the black frost filled them with a flood of words. "One way or another, the harvest will be safe," they kept saying. But señora Librada, older or more cautious, warned, "Wait till we have the wheat in the pantry before we talk about it."

For his part, the Old Ratter wasn't expecting anything from the weather. His secretiveness grew more and more sullen and intense. During the day he hardly opened his mouth and at night, when he lay down on the straw, he would invariably say to Nini, "Tomorrow we'll have to go down."

The boy restrained him: "Wait, on San Vito's day, the crayfish open."

"Crayfish!"

"It could just as well be a good year. Who knows?"

A week back, on Santa Orosia's day, matters were on the point of being resolved when Justo Fadrique the mayor, who had put on a green and red tie he wore on solemn occasions, said point-blank to the Ratter at Malvino's tavern, "Ratter, what would you say if I offered you a steady job at thirty pesetas a day plus board?"

The Ratter passed the tip of his tongue over his cracked lips. Then he roughly scratched the back of his head under his beret. It looked as though he was going to make a long speech, but he only said, "Depends . . ."

"Depends on what?"

"Depends. . . ."

"Look all you have to do is go up on the hills and dig holes with the Extremadurans." He pointed to Nini: "Of course, the kid can go with you too and eat with you."

The Ratter thought for a few moments. "All right," he said finally.

Justo Fadrique mechanically pinched his fresh-shaven chin. He'd done the same thing two afternoons before, in the city, when the lawyer said to him, "If that individual has not changed in the last few months there isn't one single reason for submitting him to a test and depriving him of his paternal rights." Now Justito looked hard at the Ratter and said with affected indifference, "The only condition is you leave the cave."

The Ratter raised his eyes. "The cave is mine," he said.

Justo Fadrique leaned on the table and added patiently, "Listen to reason, Ratter. The house at the Old Threshing Floor rents for 100 pesetas and you're going to earn 180 with board. So what do you say?"

"The cave is mine," repeated the Ratter.

Justo Fadrique extended his forearms on the tabletop and said, making an effort to soften his voice, "All right. I'll buy it from you. What do you want for it?"

"Nothing."

"Nothing? Not even a thousand?"

"No."

"But it must have a price; it must be worth something, isn't it?"

"Something."

"How much? Tell me."

The Ratter smiled slyly. "The cave is mine," he said.

Justo Fadrique shook his head and finally fixed angry eyes on the Ratter. "I could get Luisito," he said, "the fellow from Torrecillórigo, to leave your rats alone. What do you say?"

The Ratter's face became instantly transformed. His nostrils dilated and his lips clenched white. "I'll do that," he said.

Justito got up. "You haven't got the guts," he said. "In any case, think it over. If you want me to, I could help you."

From then on, the Ratter spent all his time checking the river bottom. He lived in a state of repressed excitement and at night he couldn't get to sleep. Some mornings he climbed up the Nipple of Torrecillórigo and from the top scrutinized ceaselessly the banks of the stream. At nightfall he would retire to the tavern or to the stables or to the stone bench of Antoliano's workshop. And Antoliano would say to him, "You've two hands, Ratter. Nobody needs more than that." And Rosalino would tip his head in the direction of Torrecillórigo and add, "If it were me, I wouldn't let him get away with it." Malvino at the tavern kept pushing him: "The river is yours, Ratter. Before he got his baby teeth, you were in the business."

All the while Nini was doing his best to solve the community's individual problems, but rarely did clearing a hive of drones, or castrating a boar, or weeding out the defective rabbits from a hutch earn him more than two *reales* at best. Malvino kept telling him, "Set a price, you silly kid. Don't doctors and lawyers operate that way?" Nini would shrug his shoulders and look at him with such complete aplomb that Malvino would feel uneasy and fall silent.

On San Vito's day the closed season on crayfish ended and Nini went down to the river with his multipronged hooks and his nets. He baited the hooks with worms and the nets with hunks of meat, and when the sun set he had caught five dozen or so and the crayfish were still biting hard. As night set in, the boy lit his lantern and substituted chicken guts for the meat in the nets. The crickets were singing all around and over his head; in the first of the three poplars, an owl was snapping its bill. At midnight Nini gathered up his gear, woke up the dogs, and, before returning to the cave, left a line set for eel. The crayfish were clambering about in the sack, making a wet oily clicketing.

The Old Ratter was waiting for him, sitting on his heels at the cave entrance under the kerosene lantern.

"Did you see him?" he said before Nini had clambered up to the flat spot where the thyme grew.

"No," said the boy.

The Ratter muttered something under his breath. He added: "Any crayfish?"

"Eleven and a half dozen," said Nini. And for the first time in weeks the Old Ratter's lips spread in a grin.

"If Sime doesn't fish this year, everything will be just fine," added the boy.

Sime, in past years, had been his strongest competitor. Sime went after them with her hands, tucking up her skirt and revealing her white, mottled thighs. The ball of the index finger on her right hand had a good callus and this was what she fearlessly poked into holes or into the watercress and the crayfish would grab at it with voracious delight. With such a simple technique there'd been years when Simeona had caught more than five hundred dozen. Adolfo, who drove the interurban bus, then took the crayfish to the city, sorted according to size, to sell them in the market. But this year Simeona had gone spiritual. She had let her hair hang down loose over her shoulders and encased herself in a long black robe that reached to her feet. Her garb was the same one that Eufrasia had used five years before, the first "Devotee" that the Eleventh Commandment had taken into her house. Sime, like Eufrasia, would pass three years with doña Resu, doing the most arduous and humiliating tasks, preparing herself to enter a convent. Malvino, at the tavern, was wont to say, "That's one way to get a housemaid for nothing."

The sudden change of Simeona, though, awakened the greed of the men of the town, who would use any fit occasion to ask her, "Sime, what are you going to do with the wagon?"

"I need it," was Simeona's invariable answer.

"And what are you going to do with the donkey?" they would add.

"I need him too," she replied.

Then they would scratch their heads and finally ask, "Well, can you tell me why you need a wagon and a donkey to be a nun?"

Sime answered without hesitation, "For my dowry."

For some time now Nini had been avoiding Simeona because every time she saw him she would bow her head and say, "Humiliate me." The boy would shake his head and say: "I don't know that." "Spit on me," she would add. The little boy refused. "Don't you hear me?" she would insist. "I'm telling you to spit on me. Learn to obey your elders." The boy would resist, but sometimes he'd end up pretending to. But she wasn't going to settle for that. "No, not like that. A bigger one now, and right in my face, you hear?" Other times, Sime would lie down on the ground and beg him to walk on her. Little by little the boy began to get superstitious chilly shivers every time he saw her. Most recently the girl had gotten it into her head that she was going to die, and she'd say, wringing her hands, that "it was going to come so quick she wouldn't even have time to wash." She made Nini the beneficiary of her last will. "Listen closely, Nini," she would say, "if I die I want you to have the wagon and the donkey. You sell the wagon and what you get for it you put toward masses for me. Do what you want with the donkey. You can ride him to go hunting, but every time you get on him, you remember Sime, and say an ejaculation for me."

"What's that, Sime?" the boy asked.

"My God! Are you that ignorant? An ejaculation is a short little prayer. You say, 'Lord, pardon Simeona.' Just that, you hear? But do it every time you ride the donkey, you understand that?" "Yes, Sime, don't worry," the boy assented. She stood a moment thinking and then added, "Or better still. You say every time you ride the donkey, 'Lord, pardon the sins that Sime committed with her head, then with her hands, then with her breast, then with her stomach, and like that with everything until you get to my feet.' You understand me, Nini?" Nini looked at her calmly. Finally he said, "Sime, can you commit sins with your stomach?" Suddenly Sime burst out crying. She took a while to answer him. At last she said, "Oh yes, Nini, the most serious ones. Mine was called Paquito and he's in the cemetery next to my father. Didn't you know that?" "No, Sime," replied the boy. She tossed her hair back with an impatient gesture, and said, "Of course not, you were just a little baby then."

But on San Protasio and San Tribuno's day, Sime really fell sick and Nini, seeing her sunk in the straw mattress, remembered dead Centenarian. The girl said to him, "Listen, Nini; if I die I want you to have the wagon and the donkey and Duke, you understand?"

"But Sime . . . ," the boy started to say.

"Don't give me that 'But Sime,'" she interrupted. "If I should die, I'm not going to need the dowry."

"You're not going to die, Sime. It was your father that died."

"Hush your mouth. No father dies for his child, hear?"

"All right, Sime," said the boy, intimidated.

She added, "In exchange I just ask you not to forget what I told you, remember?"

"Yes, Sime. Every time I ride the donkey I'll tell the Lord to forgive your sins beginning with your head."

Sime sighed, relieved.

"That's just right," she said. "Now, humiliate me. I don't have much time to get washed. I'm in a hurry."

"What, Sime?"

"Spit on me!" she said.

"No, Sime."

She tensed the muscles of her face. "Don't you hear me? Spit on me!"

The boy recoiled toward the door. In the sharpened features of Simeona he could now see the dead Centenarian and Grandma Iluminada. "No, I won't do it, Sime."

At that instant there filtered through the slits in the window a shrill, whining cry. Sime stopped moving, blinking her eyes nervously and, suddenly, covered her face with her hands and broke out crying hysterically. "Nini, did you hear that?" she said between two sobs. "It's the devil."

The boy came to her side. "It's an owl, Sime, don't be scared. He's hunting mice on the roof."

Then she fell back on the bed, laughed, and began to talk incoherently.

On Santa Editruda and Santa Agripina's day, Simeona was well again. Nini came across her in the square, still pale and unsteady, and for the first time since she had offered herself she didn't urge him to humiliate her. Nini asked her, "Are you all right, Sime?"

"I'm all right. Why?"

"Nothing."

They stood for a bit face to face as though trying to find out what the other was thinking. At last Nini added, "I suppose you won't go after crayfish this year, Sime?"

"Ugh!" she said. "My dear, that's all over. I'm all through with fun."

But from that night on, the crayfish became wary of Nini's hooks and nets. It was the same whether the air was still or the south or the northwest winds blew. At the end of the day the crayfish left their caves or their hiding places under the watercress and crawled around the edges of the nets, but would not decide to cross the rim. However much Nini tried, he couldn't manage to catch more than a dozen.

On his return to the cave he would say to the Old Ratter, "Sime put the evil eye on me."

The Ratter scratched himself insistently under his beret. "Nothing?" he would inquire.

"Nothing."

"We'll have to hunt rats then."

But rather than destroy the spring nests, Nini preferred to fall back on the milkweed and the lizards. He made an effort to increase his clientele by offering the milkweed from door to door. One afternoon he went to Weasel's house, although that butcher's smile terrified him.

"Matías," he said, "don't you maybe need some milkweed for your rabbits?"

"Milkweed! You're a fine one, you brat! Don't you know I got rid of my rabbits as soon as the sickness began?"

Nini blinked nervously, and suddenly Weasel grabbed

him by the collar and added, turning up his eyes as though the light bothered him, "By the way, do you know who the rascal was that let the eaglet go from the nest down in the rushes?"

"An eaglet in the rushes?" inquired Nini. "Eagles don't nest in rushes, Matías, you know that."

"Well, this time they did, see, and some *hijo de perro* cut the wire I tied the baby eagle with, what do you think of that?"

Nini shrugged his shoulders and his eyes shone bright with innocence. Matías Celemín let him go and solemnly crossed his arms on his chest. He added, "Just listen to this and let's see if you can learn your lesson once and for all. I still don't know who he is, but if someday I lay my hands on him, I'm going to smash him good until he gets over wanting to meddle where he has no business."

17

A pitiless fiery sun rose over the hilltops on the Precious Blood of Our Lord day and burned the sage and the lavender on the hillsides. In only twenty-four hours the thermometer rose above ninety-five degrees, and the valley was plunged into an enervating dog-day stupor. The hills crackled under the burning rays and the town, in the lowland, lay as though imprisoned in a cloud of suffocating dust. All around the ripe wheat was snapping while the plots of barley, which had already been mowed, with their stalks scattered among the stubble, looked like fall. Under the oven heat life languished and the infernal silence of the midday hours was barely broken by the pitiful chirping of the sparrows in the high grass along the river. As the sun went down, a lukewarm caress descended from the slopes and the townspeople took advantage of the relief to congregate at the doors of their houses and to talk quietly in small groups. From the fields the dry aroma of the grain stalks rose up, wrapped in the funereal language of the night birds, while the moths rhythmically beat against or tirelessly fluttered about the lamps in ragged orbits. From Merino Hill came the whistling of the stone curlews, and, as though under their spell, the mosquitoes sallied forth from the thick growth along the river and buzzed around with aggressive contempt. It was the end of the cycle, and as the men passed one another in the dusty streets they smiled, and their smiles were like another wrinkle in their dark faces burned by the sun and the winds of the meseta.

Nevertheless, on San Miguel de los Santos' day, the hills awoke enveloped in a sticky fog that got thicker as the day advanced. And when Pruden noticed it, he crossed the little log bridge and painfully made his way up the gully and at the flat spot where the thyme grew he shouted loudly to Nini. "Nini, boy," he said when he appeared at the cave mouth, stretching, "I don't like that haze. Do you suppose there's a chance of hail?"

Loy was sniffing the man's heels and Fa, lying flat next to the boy, was letting the boy rub her hair backward with his dirty bare foot. Nini took a good look at the horizon, with the hills lightly hazed, and finally his eyes stopped on the goshawk flapping its wings over the Nipple of Torrecillórigo. After a bit he went down the gully to the river bottom without saying a word. Pruden and the dogs were following with the same trusting docility with which the relatives of a seriously ill man follow the doctor. Once at the stream, Pruden spoke up and in a plaintive tone told Nini that the dry black-tipped wheat couldn't stand hail. As if he didn't hear, the boy proceeded to wet his middle finger and watched it carefully to see on which side it dried first. Then he slipped into the reeds and bulrushes and examined at some length their slender stems. Winged ants tirelessly clambered up the stalks and when they reached the tip would turn around and climb back down. Pruden watched him now in expectant silence and when the boy came out of the reeds he gave him a questioning look.

"There's haze and the breeze is from the south," said the boy slowly. "The winged ants are having a dance for themselves. If the wind doesn't change before noon, between now and tomorrow we'll have a thunderstorm. You'd do well to tell everybody."

But no one paid any attention to Pruden. Rosalino said, "I'm not going to start before San Auspicio's day."

"Nini says . . . ," began Pruden.

"Even though the most Holy Mary says so," cut in the foreman.

133

Nevertheless, a quarter of an hour later, when Frutos made the proclamation from the square asking for harvest hands for Pruden, the men repressed a shiver. Only Rosalino, to get the problem off his mind, made the comment, "Look, come off it, Pruden, who put that bee in your bonnet?"

But at midafternoon, a little white cloud popped over Merino Hill and after it others, denser and thicker. The men of the town couldn't take their eyes from the hill, and when it began to get dark Justito the mayor gave Frutos the order to prepare the rockets against the hail. By then the sky had completely closed in and Pruden, with Sabina, Mamertito, Little Wagger, and Críspulo, Antoliano's oldest boy, were finishing the job of putting the wheat from his field in piles. A hot wind began to blow as the sun set, and it made the unreaped fields undulate and provoked violent dust devils on the roads. The sky got gloomier and gloomier and Nini hastily gobbled up the stew the Ratter had prepared and crouched down at the door of the cave. Night had fallen suddenly and the atmosphere got thicker and thicker and unbreathable. However it was not raining yet, nor thundering, and the first flash of lightning startled the boy. Fa raised her head suddenly and growled when the rumble of the thunder came tumbling down the gully. A smell of sulfur mixed with the dry aroma of the grain stalks and the ripe wheat. The Old Ratter came to the cave mouth, looked up at the dark sky, and said, "It'll be a good one."

The hairs on Loy's back stood on end, and as the first rocket rose in the sky, aimed at the great shadowy stomach of the night, he barked angrily without knowing at what. The burst of the rocket was like the sharp cry of a child in a heated discussion among adults. After it, the sky was rent with a very bright bolt which made the range of hilltops flash as though made of silver. The thunder followed right after the lightning in a sudden fulminating blow like a whiplash. Nini said, "It's going to be worse than the one on San Zenón's day, remember?"

A second rocket was fired off from the square and another and another, continuously but without pattern, in desperation. It was like a hunter shooting pebbles with a slingshot against a herd of elephants. Another flash inundated the valley with a livid light and the noise of the thunder was followed by the moaning of the hurricane sweeping the hills and the fields, raising dense twisting clouds of dust which climbed skyward, turning in unbelievable spirals. As the wind fell, the first drops began to fall; they were big drops, swollen, like grapes, and they burst against the dried-out earth, splashing apart into tiny particles, then evaporating without leaving a trace.

The Ratter said to Nini, "It's better like this."

"What's better?"

"The rain."

"The rain?"

"Dry it would be worse."

Nini shook his head without taking his eyes off the houses in the town down below.

"It won't make any difference," he said sententiously. "The way the wheat is, it won't make any difference."

The flashes of lightning were tearing the firmament every which way, joining together in a sort of fantastic duel. The booming thunder from the northwest mingled with the flashes from the southeast and with the pattering of the hail bouncing against the tight skin of the hill like sticks beating on the head of a drum. It was hail the size of doves' eggs, but despite their size, the hailstones blew before the wind, piling up in drifts where a shrub or a depression on the hillside gave them room.

"Two hailstorms have come together," said Nini.

"Two," replied the Ratter.

"Just like in fifty-three on San Zenón's day, remember?"

"Just the same."

Little by little, the dog-day heat gave way and the invigorating breath of the damp earth rose from the stricken fields. The hail let up now and then and when it did, by the jagged light of the lightning, Nini could make out the shadowy figures of men, like mute dolls, moving about madly in the square. It wasn't just Frutos now, but Justito, and José Luis, Virgilio, Antoliano, and Matías, and Big Wagger and all the men in the town, trying to see who could launch the most rockets in a desperate attempt to drive the threat away. But the rising rockets were but an ephemeral trail, without brilliance or power, and they burst with dull pops against a low, oppressive sky. The valley round about looked ghostlike in the opaline luminosity of the lightning, and the tower of the church, the straw pile, Donalcio Hill, the Nipple of Torrecillórigo, the poplars on the riverbank, under that strange light, became phantoms, like characters in a muddled nightmare. Occasionally the showers of hail formed a solid curtain, thick and impenetrable. Nini kept saying, "It's even worse than in fifty-three."

The Ratter, motionless behind him, in the shadows, would answer, "Worse."

The fury of the heavens unleashed itself upon the valley and for five hours the sudden flashes of lightning continued and the dull reverberations of the thunder, and the pitiless hammering of the hail upon the fields. At four o'clock in the morning it suddenly stopped raining and the clouds piled up in the north, over the Nipple of Torrecillórigo, and a high, wet moon suddenly tore through the last shreds of the line squall. All the earth that the eye could see seemed to be covered with snow; and the hailstones melting on the ground made a viscous sound like that of crayfish in a basket. From time to time, behind the Nipple of Torrecillórigo, the sky was still rent with an incandescent snake, but the rumble of the thunder now took a while to arrive and it was round, uniform, without edges.

Nini went down to town as soon as it was light. The gully was wet and slippery and the boy left the path and walked along the sides to get the support of the weeds. Down below, the fields looked dead. The vegetable gardens and the three poplars on the bank timidly raised their pathetic nakedness, and the croaking of the choughs in the bays of the belltower made the great silence even more apparent. The wheat, clustered in disorder by the changing violence of the cyclone, rested gently on the mud. Here and there among the decapitated stalks, puddles gleamed. Along the roads and by the edges of the fields the bodies of corn buntings and larks lay rigidly upon the grains of wheat and the scattered shells. From the fallow fields of the Rich Man spiraling chimneys of mist rose like those the fields gave off on sunny winter days after a freezing night. A heavy smell of mud mixed with wheat stalks hung over the fields. Two magpies, emboldened by the chaos, were playing on the old horseshoeing stocks, fluffing up their feathers in the sun.

Entering the town, Nini could hear through the shutters the resigned weeping of the women. At the bottom of Pruden's backyard, half buried in the muck, was a swallow. Under the eaves, sticking their little white-black heads out the nest opening, the babies were tirelessly peeping away. The streets were deserted and in the ruts there was more mud than in midwinter. In the square señora Clo was briskly sweeping off the two steps leading to the tobacco shop. Under the thatch covering on the adobe barnyard wall was a sign in uneven letters that read, "*Viva* the draft of '56!" Loy stopped, sniffing in the entrance of José Luis' house, and Nini whistled to him softly. Señora Clo saw him then, leaned on her broom, and said to him as she moved her head up and down, biting her lower lip, "Nini, dear. What do you make of this punishment?"

"Here it is."

"Are we so bad, Nini, we have to be punished like this?"

"Must be, señora Clo."

In front of the stables, splattered with mud, the Rich Man's automobile stood, and on the same corner don Antero and several strangers were talking excitedly with the men of the town. Justito, and José Luis, and Matías Celemín, and Little Wagger, and Antoliano, and Agapito, and Rosalino, and Virgilio were all there, their eyes wide, their shoulders bent down as though under the weight of an enormous burden. And don Antero the Rich Man was saying, "We can discount the insurance. But we must not fall asleep at the switch, Justo. Right now, today, you ought to send a note requesting loans and extensions. Otherwise, it'll be the end, you hear?"

Justito agreed weakly: "I'll do what I can, don Antero, you know."

Nini passed by at a distance, the dogs close at his heels, but before he reached the vineyard, he heard Antoliano's stuttering voice: "I . . . I don't have any insurance, don Antero."

And Matías Celemín the Weasel said in strangely funereal tones, "Me either."

A rumble of voices drawn into the conversation joined Weasel like a chorus: "Me either . . . Me either . . . Me either."

On the path to the vineyard, Pruden came out to meet him. He seemed to spring from the earth like a ghost.

"Nini," he said, "I have my wheat in piles, and the kernels are still on it"—he spoke as though excusing himself—"I . . ."

The boy replied without hesitation: "Don't winnow it until it's dry," he said. "But don't put it off, because it might germinate."

Pruden grasped him by the shoulder.

"Wait," he said. "Wait. Do you think I can start winnowing and everybody else ruined?"

Nini shrugged his shoulders. Looking him calmly right in the eye, he said, "That's your business."

Pruden rubbed his hands resignedly, trying to overcome his nervousness. Then he stuck his right hand in his pocket and handed Nini a peseta.

"Take it, Nini, for what you did yesterday," he said. "I'd give you more, but I still have to pay three helpers, remember."

Going along the edge of the vineyard stripped by the

138

hailstones, Nini arrived at the river bottom. A little farther on, beyond the poplars, he came on Luis, the one from Torrecillórigo. The young man smiled at him with his bright white teeth though he kept urging on his dog.

"Go get him, go get him."

"What are you doing?"

"There's another one! Can't you see? Hunting."

"Hunting?"

"Do you think anyone can do anything else around here this year?"

He pointed at the broken wheat lying in the mud: the spacious fields converted into a sterile straw crop.

"In Torrecillórigo too?"

The man was moving along the stream keeping up with his dog, among the broken reeds. He said, "The storm didn't leave one blade of wheat standing."

The boy watched the spotted dog.

"That dog isn't trying very hard."

"Do yours do any better?"

The boy pointed to Fa's panting head: "This one's old and blind in one eye, but the pup's already had some experience and next year he'll be good at it."

The young man from Torrecillórigo burst out laughing and beat his boot with the tip of his iron bar a couple of times.

"Mine's new at it too," he said.

"He's already a year old."

"He'll be a year on San Máximo's day. How did you know?"

"By his eyes. And his mouth. What's his name?"

"Morning Star."

The boy shook his head.

"Why don't you like the name?"

"It's too long."

"Too long. What do you call yours?"

"The bitch is Fa."

"And the pup?"

"Loy."

The man laughed again. "Any name is good enough for a dog," he added ill-humoredly.

Suddenly the young man raised his eyes and his laugh pulled in around his mouth until it became a look of consternation. Nini heard hurrying footsteps and raising his eyes spied the Ratter trampling the fallen stalks of the wheat field in long strides. He was waving his iron bar in the air and shouting something inarticulate that never got to be words. Reaching the edge of the stream, he didn't stop, but leaped into the water, splashing as though impelled by some irrational force, and hurled himself upon the young man, brandishing his iron rod. Nini barely had time to get up, grab him by the worn jacket, and pull backward with all his strength. But the young man from Torrecillórigo now had hold of the Ratter's wrist, keeping the bar at a distance, while he screamed, "Listen to reason, for Christ's sake." The Ratter was muttering curses and mumbling blindly, "The rats are mine. The rats are mine!"

Suddenly Fa rushed upon the young man, angrily biting his leg, but Morning Star, in his turn, attacked the bitch, and both animals rolled off in the grass, while Loy barked excitedly, not knowing what to do. Nini, convinced of the impossibility of separating the two men, watched the rough and tumble of the fight, his eyes popping, trying to restrain the men with his shouts, but the Ratter couldn't hear him. A blind force was pushing him and as though feeding his anger he kept repeating again and again, "The rats are mine. The rats are mine."

The dogs were fighting murderously, slashing one another viciously, their bright white fangs bared, growling continuously. Once they rolled in the mud as each one got a grip on the other, and the Ratter tripped over them and fell on the wheat, with his adversary astride him. The young man from Torrecillórigo tried to overcome him by sinking his knees into Ratter's biceps, and as he strained his utmost he kept muttering, "Lis-ten-to-rea-son-for-Chris-sake!" But the Ratter got the better of him; he arched his